PRAISE FOR *WILD*

★ "An intense tale of survival and action. A must-have."
—*School Library Journal*, starred review

★ "Short chapters, outstanding cover art,
and a breathless pace. Outstanding suspense."
—*Kirkus Reviews*, starred review

★ "Action lovers will relish every word.
With *Wildfire*—reminiscent of *Hatchet* and the real-life
saga *Lost on a Mountain in Maine*—Philbrick transforms
a raging inferno into an impressively plotted escape story
full of heart and soul." —*BookPage*, starred review

PRAISE FOR *ZANE AND THE HURRICANE: A STORY OF KATRINA*:

★ "An appropriately serious and occasionally gruesome
tale of surviving Hurricane Katrina, buoyed by large doses
of hope and humor." —*Kirkus Reviews*, starred review

WILDFIRE

WILDFIRE

A NOVEL

Rodman Philbrick

Scholastic Inc.

Many thanks to my hotshot friends, Eric Metcalf, David Carr, and Teddy Bryan, for their fascinating accounts of fighting wildfires in the Bitterroot, in Montana.

ISBN 978-1-338-71364-0

10 9 8 7 6 5 4   21 22 23 24 25

Printed in in the U.S.A.   40
This edition first printing 2021

Special thanks to Jazan Higgins, who cares so deeply about reading.

Book design by Nina Goffi

In memory of Sean Charles Pearl

Day One

7 a.m. broadcast from radio station WRPZ, 98.6 FM

"Good morning, campers! This is a wake-up call for my friends at Camp Wabanaski, as requested. Hey, kids, it's gonna be another day without rain—sixty-five days and counting! The hottest, driest summer ever recorded! Temps in the mid-nineties yet again. Hot enough to burn, baby, burn. That's according to the Maine Forest Service, so please, no open fires! Only thing we'll be burning around here is classic vinyl, deep in the groove with your host, Phat Freddy Bell, broadcasting from high atop the lowest official mountain in the great state of Maine.

"Rise and shine, campers! Rise and shine!"

1.

When Trees Explode

We wake up to the smell of smoke. At first it isn't too bad, but then the smoke starts to sting and makes our eyes water, and by the time breakfast is over, the counselors say a decision has been made. The fire is still far away enough that we can't see it yet, but to be on the safe side, Camp Wabanaski will be evacuated as soon as the buses get here.

The smoke is getting worse, a layer of stinky fog that dims the sky. Except along the horizon, which is suddenly flickering orange above the treetops.

Wildfire, moving fast.

"The buses have arrived!" a counselor shouts. "Grab your gear and board! Remain calm but move quickly!"

We're only allowed one bag, so I jam everything into my hiking pack.

I'm on the second step of the bus, tight in a line of super-excited campers, when I remember my phone is still on the charger. I need it to call Mom and let her know I'm okay. I manage to sneak off without catching the attention of the staff, scoot around the buses, and race back to the cabin.

Sprint down the trail, by the tall white pines clustered around the sign for Camp Wabanaski, "A Summer Experience." Turn left at the intersection for Lake Path, then right on Cabin Path, and there it is, dead ahead, my cabin.

Inside, the smoke is even thicker. My throat is starting to burn, like I gargled something nasty.

Phone, phone, where's the phone?! Should be on the rickety table next to the wake-up radio, but it isn't.

Should I run back to the bus and hope for the best? Answer: yes!

Then I spot a phone under the table. Blue rubber case, labeled with my name, Sam Castine. Grab it up, slip it into my back pocket, and bolt. Screen door slamming like a gunshot behind me.

Whoa! Serious smoke! The buses are no longer visible through the trees, it's that thick. But I don't need to see the buses, I know my way back to the entrance area where they're parked. I have a really good sense of direction. My dad used to say I was born with a compass in my head. Not that I need a compass. All I have to do is follow the trails, Cabin Path to Lake Path, and I'll be there.

What stops me is a flash of heat. Feels like an oven door has opened over my head. I look up and see something astonishing. The cluster of tall white pines blooming orange flower blossoms from the top. No, that's wrong. Not flowers. Flames. Flames pouring from branch to branch like a gleaming waterfall of fire. Fat flaming drops dripping on the grass below the pines, igniting it instantly.

The pines explode and disintegrate. A wave of flame erupts from the base of the tree trunks, setting up a wall of fire between me and the buses. A wall of fire that wants to kill me.

There's only one thing to do.

Run the opposite way.

Run for my life.

2.

Run, Boy, Run

Remember me bragging about having a compass in my head? Ha. Must be that fear turns it off, because I've got no idea where I am in the world. Somewhere inside the smoke, running away from the heat, like a bug trying to find its way off a hot light bulb. Lungs burning, eyes blinded by the hot, itchy smoke, and the only thought in my head is run, run, run.

Smashing through low pine branches that reach out like scratchy hands. Fighting through sap-drenched undergrowth that grabs my feet. Somewhere along the way, I drop the bulky backpack. Too heavy, too awkward. Keep light, keep moving. Faster. Gotta go faster.

run

gasp

run

gasp

Don't think, don't try to figure anything out, because it takes too much energy. If you want to live, you gotta run, boy, run.

Not enough air in the smoke. Can't breathe, it hurts too much. Iron bands tightening around my lungs, choking me down.

On my knees. Can't breathe. Can't run.

Dying?

Maybe. Probably.

What saves me is a gust of wind. I'm on my hands and knees in the weeds, desperately trying to find enough air for one last breath, when something changes.

The wind. It had been behind me, driving the flames, when suddenly it shifts. In an instant the smoke lifts, and through tear-blurred eyes I can see again.

I'm in a patch of low, woodsy undergrowth, surrounded by whip-thin birch trees. Beyond the birch trees, the ground dips into a shallow swamp.

Yes.

Get to the swamp while you have the chance, while you can think.

Crawl, boy, crawl.

No, must go faster! I stagger to my feet, take a deep breath of that fresh, lifesaving wind in my face, and aim for the swamp.

3.

Your Son Is Missing

Not sure how long I stay there, lying in the muddy, tea-colored water with my back against a rotting stump. The swamp isn't very deep. Less than a foot. Barely a swamp at all. Probably the drought has dried it out. But the forest is much thinner, and I can see a chunk of sky, gray and glaring. The stench of smoke is harsh, but it no longer hurts to breathe, and the hot wind stays strong. Maybe the shift in wind turned the fire back, or maybe the fire just decided to go somewhere else.

Whatever, it's good to be alive. Gives me time to think and plan. How do I find my way back to Camp Wabanaski? Does it still exist? Last time I saw the camp, before the curtain of smoke came down, it was inside the fire. Trees exploding. Old wooden cabins, they must have gone off like popcorn.

What about the buses, did they get away in time? And if they did, did anybody notice I'm not there? Will they notify my mom? Sorry, Mrs. Castine, your son is missing and presumed burnt to a crisp.

My phone! Went to all that trouble and almost forgot. Mom won't have access to family or friends for the first ten days of treatment, but I can leave a message with the staff. Then it hits me like a slap to the head. The phone is in my back pocket. And I'm sitting in swampy water.

I roll over, grab the slippery phone, and desperately try to dry it off. Blowing on the screen and muttering, "Come on, come on. Please work, please!"

Drips of swamp water ooze from a crack in the screen. That can't be good.

"One last call," I beg, and hold the button in.

Waiting for the symbol to come up.

Waiting. Waiting.

Nothing.

I lift the phone up to the sky, hoping against hope, but the screen stays dark. That's bad, but it gets even worse. When I try to put the phone back in my pocket, it slips away, vanishing into the tea-colored water. I paw through the muck, splashing swamp goo, going, "No, no, no, no! Please, no!"

But it's too late. Way too late. Even if I managed to retrieve it, the phone is for sure ruined by now, if it hadn't been already.

I want to cry like a baby, I really do, but the heat of the fire has dried the tears right out of me.

Forget the phone. Find your way to a road and get yourself home.

Slogging out of the mucky water, I follow along the edge of the swamp.

4.

Don't Believe in Sorry

My dad had a saying he got from some old TV show. *Let's be careful out there.* He always said it with half a laugh, but he meant it, whether we were going camping or hiking or whatever. If he could see me somehow, that's what he'd say: *Be careful out there, boy.* And maybe he'd add another of his favorites: *Make a plan and stick to it.* Something like that.

Easier said than done, but I'll try.

The swamp I'm following gets narrower and narrower, until finally it becomes nothing more than a dark path, a layer of rotting leaves and pine needles. I keep looking over my shoulder, checking to make sure the fire isn't catching up. So far so good.

Now, if only I can find a road. A road means passing vehicles, maybe even a police car. They'll be evacuating the whole area, right? Somebody is bound to see me. Somebody will have a phone so I can let Mom know I'm okay.

So be careful. And the plan? The plan is simple: Keep walking until you find a road, and hope fire doesn't get in your way.

When the last trace of the swamp disappears, I pick a direction and stick to it as best I can. Trying to follow a straight line through the forest, going from tree to tree. Worst thing you can do, lost in the woods, is start circling.

Hours go by. Or that's how it feels. Without the phone, I have no way of telling time. Not much of the sky is visible under the canopy of the forest, but I'm pretty sure the sun is lower. Which probably means it's afternoon. The clock in my stomach is letting me know I'm hungry and thirsty, that I haven't eaten or had anything to drink since early morning.

The thirsty part is the worst. I keep thinking if only I'd managed to hang on to my backpack, I'd have a couple of water bottles, two energy bars, and dry clothing. My throat is so parched I'm starting to regret not drinking that stinky swamp water when I had the chance. Should I turn around and retrace my steps?

No. Because that would mean heading back in the direction of the fire. Stick to the plan. Be on the lookout for a brook or a stream. Which normally wouldn't be hard to find, but this is the year of the drought. No rain for months. Heat-wave hot for weeks. All but the biggest rivers have shriveled to nothing.

Hot, hot, hot. My throat and mouth feel like dry, gritty dirt. My eyes are so dry they're scratchy. Get to a road, boy. Someone will stop, give you water. Drink first, then borrow a phone.

Maybe I should take a nap.

Wow! Where did that come from? Taking a nap in the woods with wildfires raging only a few miles away, that's like the worst idea in the world. Forget about napping. Forget you're tired and thirsty. Keep moving. Find a road, get rescued, and drink a gallon of icy cold water.

Maybe just lie down for a minute.

No, no, no. Absolutely not! Keep going!

Thirsty and tired don't matter. Humans survive for days without water. Banish water from your mind. Concentrate on finding a road.

When I was really little, three or four, I used to sleepwalk. I'd be sound asleep in my bed, and the next thing I knew, my parents would find me in the living room or the kitchen or the hallway, just standing there, still asleep. Weird, huh? Like something in my dreams made me get up and wander.

That's what it feels like, trudging through the forest. Like I'm somewhere between awake and asleep. My legs keep walking, but part of me is floating along, like a balloon on a string.

Something about being in the woods brings up a memory of Dad taking me trout fishing, the year before he went to Afghanistan. Baxter State Park, which is huge. We hiked five miles from a parking lot to this fishing spot Dad knew about from when he was my age. His father took him, so this was like a family tradition. Told me I would always remember my first trout stream, even if we didn't catch fish. But we did catch fish. We caught eleven brook trout and kept five to eat over a campfire. So that was the year my father taught me how to cast with a fly rod—I sucked, actually—and build a campfire, and whittle with a jackknife, and how to read a trail map, and a lot of cool, outdoorsy stuff. He promised when I was twelve he'd take me duck hunting, but he never came back from Afghanistan, so that was that.

What would he think of me wandering through the woods with no idea of direction, or where to go, or how to get there? His boy who was supposed to have a compass in his head?

Sorry, Dad.

Sorry, sorry, sorry.

I can almost hear him saying, *Don't give me sorry, boy. I don't believe in sorry,* which was another saying of his, when I notice the ground feels different under my feet. Which kind of snaps me back into paying attention. Looking down, I see a tire track in the dirt. No, wait, two of them, running in parallel. Tracks from a good-sized vehicle, like maybe a big truck.

A road!

5.

Beautiful Music

Okay, let's be clear. What I've stumbled upon is an old logging road, not much wider than a trail. Cut through the forest long ago, to bring out lumber. How do I know that? Because my dad was a trucker, and when he was young, he drove for paper companies in Skowhegan, hauling pulpwood out of the forest and taking it to the mills for processing. Dangerous work, driving heavily loaded trucks on dirt trails. Make a mistake and the truck can flip over, with all those heavy logs crushing the cab.

This particular road is pretty overgrown. Looks like it hasn't been used in years. So it's not like I can stick out my thumb and hitch a ride. On the other hand, I'm pretty sure that logging roads eventually connect with a main road. They'd have to, to bring the wood to the paper mill, right? So it's really important that I choose the right direction. Go the wrong way, the old road will likely take me deeper into the woods.

Which way? I've no idea. How could I?

Make your decision and stick to it.

15

Thanks, Dad, but that doesn't really help.

In the end, I flip a coin in my head and turn left.

The old trail winds through the forest, under a canopy of green leaves. Mossy, rotting stumps squat alongside the old trail, more proof that loggers worked this road, back in the day. A lot of the paper mills have closed, which is why my father switched over to bulk tanker trucking before I was born. Hauled everything from milk to gasoline. Made a good living, but nothing like the money they paid him to drive gas tankers in Afghanistan, for as long as it lasted. Combat pay, even though he was a civilian. Money intended for my college fund, and to save for a bigger house, so I'm at least partly to blame for why he took the job in the first place.

But I'd rather not think about that. Concentrate on covering ground while I've got the chance. The light is dim, this far into the woods, and getting dimmer. And the thirst is starting to make me feel light-headed. They say being dehydrated can mess with your mind, and thinking straight will help me stay alive. So I need to find water, and fast.

There has to be water in leaves, right? A drop or two. Tearing a few leaves off a bush, I stuff them into my mouth and chew. Not to swallow, just to squeeze a little moisture into my mouth and throat. But the taste is so awful I try to spit it out, and a piece of leaf sticks to the back of my throat and makes me gag and cough. And cough some more. When it finally comes loose, I'm able to catch my breath.

That coughing fit makes me stop and remember something important we learned in camp. When you're lost in the woods, you have to think and plan, or risk dying of exposure, which can happen if your body temperature gets out of whack, too hot or cold, or if you don't get enough water.

Use your brain or die, that's the rule.

Our camp counselor explained the danger, but most of us already knew. Every year tons of hikers and hunters get lost in the woods of Maine, and we hear about it on TV. Usually they get rescued, but not always. Which makes me remember one of those stories, about a Girl Scout who got separated from her troop on a foggy day, and how she found water by following the mosquitoes. Because mosquitoes are never far from water.

Smart girl.

Never before have I wanted to get bit by mosquitoes. But here I am, trudging along an old logging road in the dying light, so thirsty it hurts. If getting bit by a few mosquitoes is what it takes to find water, so be it.

Come for me, you whiny little monsters. Lead me to water. Lead me to life.

I never do get bit. But as I concentrate on listening for the annoying, telltale whine of a mosquito, I hear something

17

much, much better. A sound more beautiful than music. The gurgle of running water.

It's coming from deep in the brush, just off the logging trail. I approach slow and careful. Thinking about snakes, if you must know. There are no poisonous snakes in Maine, according to our camp counselor, but I don't care to meet one, poisonous or not.

What I find looks at first like the stump of a giant tree surrounded by thick green ferns. But it turns out it's actually an old spring. The low, circular sides are mossy bricks that look like wood in the dim light. The top is a big round cover made of thick, rough-sawn planks. Part of the brick siding has crumbled away, and that's where the water is leaking out, feeding the ferns.

By then I'm on my hands and knees, mouth jammed up against those mossy bricks, slurping down cool, clear water. Beautiful water. Blessed water. Best-tasting water that ever there was.

I drink until my belly is full, tight as a drum, and I'm woozy with the thrill of it. So satisfied that I'm tempted to curl up next to the spring and go to sleep. Might have done it, too, if a thought didn't bob to the surface and fight for attention.

What's a man-made spring doing in the middle of nowhere? The brick sides and thick wooden cover had been built for a purpose, to keep the water clean and contained. Shift that cover, and water could be drawn out by the bucketful. But why here, and for who?

Only one answer makes sense. The spring was built for the same men who had cut this logging road into the woods. Lumbermen from the lumber camps. Which gets me back on my feet and hurrying along the trail with hope in my heart.

6.

Sleep Like the Dead

The old lumber camp is nearly invisible in the fading light. Located not fifty yards from the spring, in a clearing overgrown with bushes, ferns, and skinny saplings that makes everything look blended together. Kind of a natural camouflage. I can barely make out a couple of long, low sheds slowly sinking into the ground. One of them has a caved-in roof. Nearby is a small, one-story cabin, roof intact.

The little cabin is not much bigger than a garden shed, but it can be shelter for the night. A place to hide from bears. Did I mention bears? My dad said steer clear of bears, if possible. Mostly a black bear will leave you alone, he said, but not always. Especially a mama bear with cubs. Very dangerous. So bears have been on my mind ever since the sun started setting. And when you're thinking about bears, every clump of bushes looks like one, ready to charge.

I hurry across the clearing and get to the sagging front porch of the cabin just as darkness falls like a hot, steamy blanket. I can barely make out the front door, and expect to find it locked. Maybe I can skinny through a window? Or break in if necessary—this is an emergency, what with the wildfire coming to get me if the wind shifts. But when I thumb the latch, the door swings creakily inward.

"Anybody home?" I call into the darkness, not really expecting a reply. The air inside is hot and stale and smells of wood and pinesap. Sweat trickles down my forehead and stings my eyes. Sweat from the heat, but also from being afraid, spooked by the dark, and terrified the fire will catch up.

I feel along the wall beside the front door, hoping for a light switch. No luck. Doubtful the cabin has electricity. I sure didn't see any power lines nearby. As I search for a light switch, something hard and solid bumps my wrist. It's all I can do not to scream. Was that a bony hand?

My heart is slamming so hard I can barely breathe.

Don't be a moron, Sam! Don't panic. Keep it together. Use your brain. Find what bumped you and deal with it. Slowly I pass my fingers along the wall and touch the thing that nearly scared me to death.

A flashlight hanging from a thin rope, just inside the door.

I press the button, expecting the batteries to be long dead. But to my amazement, a beam of light nearly blinds me.

I've never been so grateful for such a small thing. A simple flashlight. "Thank you," I say, to whoever was thoughtful enough to leave it hanging by the door. "Thank you, thank you, thank you."

The warm beam of the flashlight lights up a small, tidy interior. A potbellied cast-iron woodstove with a tin chimney going up through the roof. A little square table with two spindly chairs. A narrow bunk. A stack of wooden crates piled up against the back wall. And dust, lots of dust.

I check out the top crate. Plastic gallon jugs of supermarket water. The labels haven't faded or peeled, so they can't be that old. The lumber camp looks abandoned, like the logging is long over, but it seems like someone has visited this cabin recently. Which explains the flashlight, the fresh jugs of water.

A supply of water is good—no, it's great, it's amazing—but I'm suddenly so exhausted I can barely keep my eyes open. I head for the narrow bunk. Thin mattress, no sheets, but I'm grateful to have a bed.

Doesn't matter that the cabin is stifling hot, and smells old and musty, but at least it doesn't stink of smoke. A safe place to sleep seems like a treasure I couldn't imagine when the flames were chasing me from tree to tree. As soon as the sun rises, I intend to keep running, putting distance between me and the fire. But tonight I need to get some rest.

I lie in the dark, wishing I were home. My mom and I live in Wells, Maine. Not in the beachy, touristy part, but out in the woods by the sandpits. Which is fine. I like it out there.

At night you can hear the coyotes yipping under the power lines. Yipping and howling and singing to each other. Kind of scary if you never heard it before, but once you know, it's like listening to a family conversation. Dad, Mom, and the kids.

I miss it, miss it, miss it.

I fall asleep worrying about my mother. Did the people at the clinic tell her I was missing? Will she stay in the program? Or will she quit and try to find me on her own?

I can hear myself begging her: *Twenty-eight days, Mom, that's all you have to do. Four weeks and then you'll be free. No more pills. Your mind will be clear. I'll go to summer camp, and you'll go to rehab. They'll help you, Mom, I promise. Stay in the program, please?*

No more pills, no more pills, no more pills. Pray for no more pills.

I sleep like the dead.

Day Two

7.

Make a Giant "HELP"

Where am I? That's my first thought as I wake up. I take a deep breath of hot, stuffy air and look around. Oh yeah. The little cabin in the abandoned lumber camp. I sniff the air, but the smell of a distant fire hasn't changed. My second thought is about my mother. I'm worried. Did I mention she's in rehab?

Maybe you think all drug addicts are losers. Not my mother. A loser would give up when her husband dies in some stupid road accident on the other side of the world. A few days after the funeral, she called me into the kitchen and sat me down. "I'm not sure what's next for us, Sammy, but it will be something good, that's a promise. Your dad is gone, and we'll miss him every day, but that doesn't mean we give up. No way, not ever. Not as long as we have each other."

Mom was sad about Dad, desperate sad, but she kept her job as a physical therapist, taking extra shifts to make ends meet. In her free time, which wasn't much, she made sure I was okay, and worked in her garden, which she always said was better than medicine.

Weeding, planting, helping things bloom, helping people heal. That's my mother, or it was until she got rear-ended in a parking lot last year and injured her neck real bad, and started taking prescription meds for the pain. After a while she was taking more and more pills, and pretty soon it seemed like she wasn't really there, like she couldn't concentrate or pay attention. She started missing shifts and let the garden go to weeds.

Mom kept apologizing, and blamed it on being tired, but it kept getting worse. Until one day I came home from school and found her passed out on the floor, barely breathing. I tried to wake her, and when that didn't work, I dialed 911 and they took her to the hospital and pumped her stomach and tested her blood for opioids.

Opioids. I hate that word. Sounds like some horrible kind of mind spider that takes over your brain. Anyhow, at the hospital, they assigned me a social worker, Mrs. Labrie, who talked to me about going into foster care while my mother went to rehab. When I freaked out, she came up with a plan for me to go to summer camp instead. Which was the perfect solution, until the fire wrecked everything.

I swing my legs over the steel-frame bunk. Sitting there all sweaty with the stifling heat as I try to clear my head. Think smart, like my dad used to say. Stop worrying about things I can't change. Nothing I can do about Mom, not today. Today I need to keep clear of the fire and find my way back home. Concentrate on making that happen.

I have no idea what time it is, but it must be early, not long after sunrise. I'm dizzy, or maybe light-headed is more like it. The constant heat is partly to blame, but mostly it's because my belly is growling, *Feed me, feed me.* I head for the stack of crates, figuring to fill up on bottled water. But what I find in the second crate is way better than that. The crate is loaded with canned goods. B&M beans, Dinty Moore beef stew, canned franks and beans, canned brown bread, Spam, pears, tuna fish. Tons of stuff, enough to live for weeks or maybe months, and there's even a can opener and a jackknife!

Cold beef stew for breakfast, right out of the can? If you haven't eaten for twenty-four hours, it tastes great, let me tell you. And better yet, the food goes right to my brain, and out pops an idea. Okay, maybe it's not an original idea, but it just might work. Remember that movie where a guy gets stranded on an island and spells out "HELP" in the sand? What if I do the same thing in the clearing, except spell it out with trees? Not big trees, of course, but white birch saplings small enough for me to drag into place?

I mean, they'll be searching for me, right? Sending out helicopters and planes and search parties, whatever they do when a kid goes missing in the woods. Unless they think I burned up in the fire. Which is discouraging for about ten seconds, and then I decide to make a giant "HELP" and hope for the best. That somebody will see it and rescue me before the fire gets here. Before the old camp explodes in flames, and me with it.

29

So my plan is to find an ax or a handsaw and get started. Doesn't take long to search the little cabin and discover there's nothing bigger than the jackknife I found. I decide to put it in my pocket and hope the owner won't mind. Then I remember those falling-down sheds. It makes sense there might be old hand tools in a lumber camp, and if there are, they'd likely be stored in a shed.

Feeling like the smartest twelve-year-old in the universe, I stride out of the hot cabin and into the overgrown clearing. I check out the skyline, looking for signs of fire. The horizon is dark with smoke, but it still looks a long way off. Shoving my way through low bushes and ferns, I head for the closest shed. The one where the roof is more or less intact.

The big shed doors are heavy, but swing smoothly on recently oiled hinges. A blast of super-hot air hits me from inside, and a faint odor of something familiar. Gasoline and motor oil. In my mind, that means a chain saw, which would make my job a whole lot easier. If I can figure out how to start a chain saw. Can't be that hard, right?

As the doors swing all the way open, daylight spreads into the dim interior of the shed. And what I see there just about blows my mind.

8.

The Promise He Made Me

The thing is covered by a dust sheet, but I can sort of make out the shape. A vehicle. Could be an off-road four-wheeler, but I don't think so. Too wide. Only one way to find out.

I take a corner of the dust sheet and pull it away.

"Whoa," I say, amazed. "No way!"

The thing under the sheet is a Jeep. An old Jeep, like from the wars in the last century. Dull green in color and as stocky as a bulldog, with thick tires and old leather seats and no doors, and a flat, tilt-down windshield. There's a shovel and ax attached to the passenger side, and a couple of five-gallon fuel cans strapped to the back bumper. No ignition or key that I can see, just a simple lever marked *Off/On*, and a small compass mounted on the dash.

You may be wondering, what's the big deal about finding an old Jeep, instead of, say, a nice new four-wheeler? Because of my dad, that's why. His favorite vehicle of all time was an Army Jeep! His grandfather drove one in World War II. In one story, the old man had gotten stuck behind enemy lines in the Battle of the Bulge, but he escaped because of his Jeep—rescuing four wounded soldiers along the way.

I watched a lot of WWII movies with Dad, who wanted to pass along our family history. Plus, it was fun watching movies with him because he knew so much about it all.

Once I asked him if he'd get me a Jeep when I turned sixteen. That made him laugh. "You're only eight years old," he said.

"That makes me halfway there."

He laughed even harder.

"Promise? Swear-on-your-heart promise?"

"Tell you what, Scamp," he said. "I promise that someday we'll buy an old Jeep and fix it up, you and me."

"When?"

"When we can afford it, and that's the end of this conversation."

But it wasn't the end, not by a long shot. Whenever I saw an old Army-style Jeep on the road or in a yard, we'd talk about how someday we'd get one of our own. *I wish you could see this, Dad! You'd already have the hood up.*

What I find in the old Jeep's little glove compartment makes it even better. There's a neatly folded map that looks well used. A small gray plastic folder contains a vehicle registration in the name of Aldrich Brown, and a faded black-and-white photo of a tall, lean man in an Army uniform standing next to a Jeep. Maybe he owns the lumber camp property, or has permission to store a vehicle here. Maybe he's the one who keeps the cabin stocked with provisions. Whatever, he has a big grin on his face. I turn the photo over and there, in neat handwriting, are the words *U.S. Army, 40th Infantry, Korea 1952.*

Cool! I'm so focused on the Jeep, and on memories of my dad, that at first I don't notice the smell. The terrible smell. The awful, terrifying smell. Then it hits me, and I run out of the shed and look to the sky, which is suddenly boiling dark clouds and flashing orange along the tree line.

The fire is suddenly close and getting closer. The wind has shifted, and it carries the heat and stink of fire.

My heart sinks. The wildfire is back with a vengeance, driving the hot sparky wind, and there's no time to make a plan. I thought the worst was over, but obviously not. All I can do is get moving as quickly as possible, and try and keep ahead of the flames behind the boiling smoke. Smoke that's already burning my throat.

Water. I'm going to need water. Best I can do is grab a few jugs for the road. Go. Make it fast. Don't mess it up like you did going back for the stupid phone.

I'm sprinting for the little cabin, when animals suddenly explode from the surrounding forest. Birds are first, hundreds of them, streaking across the clearing. Big black crows, tiny bright songbirds, and eerie-looking owls, silent but for the swoop of their wings. I raise my arms to cover my head, afraid they'll peck my eyes out, but the birds avoid me and rush up into the smoke-darkening sky.

Next come squirrels, tails flattened as they skitter through the underbrush, chittering with fear. Then ground-hogs waddling along, and raccoon families screeching, and other close-to-the-ground creatures running so fast they're blurred. Weasels, maybe.

Last is a young deer with a rack of mossy antlers. He enters the clearing in one mighty leap, freezing for a split second, as if posing for an amazing nature picture, and then vanishes into a stand of pines on the opposite side of the camp.

The message couldn't be clearer. *Run.* If you want to live, *run.*

I kick open the cabin door and grab crates of cans and jugs of water. I race back to the shed, fear choking my throat. Because I can hear the fire now, roaring close behind the thick wall of smoke. The crackle of burning branches. The whoosh of leaves igniting into flames. It can only mean one thing: Fire is eating the forest. Fire is coming so fast I can't possibly outrun it. Not without help. Not without the Jeep.

Doesn't matter that I don't know how to drive, it's my only chance.

9.

Between the Fire and Me

I toss the crates into the back of the Jeep and slip behind the wheel, hands shaking. Trying to remember what little I know about driving a standard transmission. I know the clutch is important. That's how you shift gears. But which one is the clutch pedal and which is the brake?

Take a guess. I press down on the left pedal. It goes all the way to the floor. Okay, that must be the clutch. I turn the lever on the dash to *On*.

Nothing. Total silence. I jiggle the lever. Still nothing.

Forget the Jeep. Run for your life.

No, wait. *Starter pedal?* Yes! Remember? Dad said really old Jeeps had a starter pedal. Something you had to press down with your foot. To make the engine turn over.

Find it, boy. Find it or die.

I look down and spot a small, knobby rubber pedal. I press on it with my foot. The most amazing thing happens: The engine turns over and catches!

Nothing ever sounded so good as that engine purring.

Like it woke up happy from a deep sleep and is ready to get to work.

That running engine gives me hope, but the smoke is getting thicker, filling the shed. My eyes sting.

What do I do next? How do I make it go?

My brain screams, "JUST DO SOMETHING, YOU IDIOT! Put this beast in gear and get moving!"

Yes! But how? There are two stick shifts! One big and one small! One for regular and one for four-wheel drive? The bigger stick must be for regular transmission, right? But how do I get it into first gear?

Then I see it. A diagram on the dashboard. First gear is to the left and down.

Quick! Do it or get burned to a crisp!

I grab the stick, pull it left and down. It clicks into place. Okay. Now put your right foot on the gas pedal and lift the clutch pedal with your left. Careful! Don't stall the engine!

My left foot accidently slips off the clutch pedal and *WHAM!* there's an awful grinding noise as the Jeep lurches into gear. Suddenly we're out of the shed, me and the Jeep. Bouncing through the clearing, knocking down bushes and skinny saplings with fire raging behind us.

I'm fighting to get control. The steering wheel bucks in my sweaty hands like a thing alive. I manage to grab hard enough so it stops slipping through my fingers.

I'm in control, more or less. I'm steering for the path, steering for my life. Because the fire behind me is louder than the engine in front of me.

Drive, boy, drive! Go! Go! Go!

I know this sounds crazy, but as me and that old Jeep tear through the clearing, I'm laughing out loud. The vehicle is bucking like a horse, fighting to go wild, and I'm howling in relief. Hanging on to that steering wheel like my life depends on it. Because guess what? It does!

I sneak a look behind just in time to see the lumber camp explode into fire. The sheds are burning, dripping with flames. The birches are going up like skinny white candles, spreading from tree to tree. There are hot threads of red and orange glowing behind the smoke. It would look beautiful if it wasn't so awful.

When I get to the old logging trail, I have to choose which way to go. Right or left? Instinct tells me I need to head into the wind. So I steer to the left. The Jeep finds the ruts, and the steering wheel stops fighting me so much. Like it knows the way.

Maybe it does. No, that's crazy, it's just a machine. Nuts and bolts and steel. It feels alive because the trail is so bumpy, and because my heart is beating hard enough for two. I'm super frightened and super excited at the same time. The fire scares me half to death, but driving the Jeep is the most fun I've ever had. The farther we get down the trail, the less smoke in the air. I'm feeling more confident.

I'd like to turn around and check what's happening behind me. Is the fire catching up? But I don't dare take my eyes off the old logging trail. What would Dad say? Keep the wheels in the ruts! Don't stop, because what if you can't get it into gear again? That would be fatal. Got to keep moving.

Yes, Dad, yes. Put as much distance as possible between the fire and me.

I'm pedal to the metal in first gear. I could try for second gear and get more speed, but what if it stalls? And I'm bouncing so hard I'm not sure I can handle going faster. Every now and then we hit a root or rock that makes the steering wheel shudder, and the Jeep groans, like it feels pain.

I decide not to change anything, just stick with it for now. Try not to worry about what's happening behind me. My mission is to keep it on the path. Dad was always saying, *Learn as you go*, right? So now's my chance. Stay focused, pay attention, and let the vehicle eat up the yards.

Not sure how long it lasts, that first part of the journey. Half an hour? Maybe seven miles down the trail? I'm drenched in sweat, but we're doing great, the Jeep and me. And we might have got clear of the fire for good, if it wasn't for what happened next.

10.

The Girl with the Raccoon Eyes

The first screech sounds like a wounded bird. It calls again, closer and louder. Not a bird. It's human. Definitely human.

I put the Jeep in neutral and roll to a stop, listening.

"Hey!" comes a faint voice. "Hey, you! Wait, please wait!"

A girl. At first I can't see her. Then she pushes her way through the tree branches, maybe fifty yards from the logging road. Limping along as fast as she can, leaning on a stick, with a small backpack slung over her shoulder. Face covered with soot, except for her eyes. Makes her look like a reverse raccoon.

I leave the engine running and get out to help. She stumbles through the ferns, hurrying like she's afraid I'll leave her behind. I give her a shoulder to lean on. Not sure it helps, because she's a head taller than me.

Boy, does she stink of smoke and sweat.

"It almost got me," she says, panting. "The fire last night. I ran and I ran. No idea where I was going. Just trying to get away."

"You're okay."

I guide her to the Jeep.

She collapses into the passenger seat and starts to cry. Great, heaving sobs of relief. She wipes tears and soot from her face with the back of her hand. "Sorry. Sorry. I don't cry. Well, hardly ever. But I thought I was dead. And then I heard that beautiful motor sound. I was so afraid it would pass by before I could find it. Ran as hard as I could, until I tripped and hurt my ankle."

"But you kept on running."

"I guess." She focuses on me, as if seeing me for the first time. "Excuse me, but are you old enough to drive?"

"I'm doing okay."

"You're what, twelve?"

"Almost thirteen. Do you want a ride or not?"

That makes her laugh. "Ha! Sorry for asking. It's not like there's any cops around to give you a ticket."

"Fire's coming this way. We best keep moving." I get behind the wheel, put the Jeep in gear. "Um, there's a jug of water in the back seat. Help yourself."

Up until three minutes ago, I was on my own, the only human in the woods, or that's how it felt. I kind of liked it that way. Then this girl appears out of nowhere. Delphy Pappas. She's from Camp Calusa, down the lake from Camp

Wabanaski. Two years older than me, broad-shouldered and way taller, with a long dark ponytail. She's big. Strong and solid. The kind of girl you'd want on your sports team. As we bounce along the ruts, keeping a steady pace, she raises her voice above the noise of the engine and thanks me for stopping.

"No problem."

"Is this your Jeep?" she asks. "What are you doing out here?"

I tell her about going back for my phone and missing the bus and stumbling into the lumber camp. "That's where I found the Jeep. It saved my life. And I guess I saved it, too, because the lumber camp went up in flames. What about you?"

She looks away. "I was, ah, out in the woods the night before the fire."

"Yeah?"

"I was, um, texting someone. Then it was really late and I got totally lost in the dark. Had to drink water from this disgusting mucky pool. Next morning—yesterday, right?—I could see the camp through the trees when the sun came up. Almost made it."

"The fire. It came wicked fast."

She nods quickly. "All I could do was run. Never been so scared in my life."

"Calusa, that's a survival camp, right?"

"Fitness. Mostly sports. For me, it was track and volley-ball. Which I guess probably saved my life. The running part. So where are we heading?"

"I don't know, exactly. I'm hoping this trail connects with a main road, and we get there before the fire does."

"Okay," says the girl with the raccoon eyes. "Hope is good."

11.

Dead as a Doornail

We rumble along for at least an hour, making good progress—the smoke has thinned from the sky and the smell is fainter by the minute. I'm getting more relaxed and confident behind the wheel. I've got this thing beat. I can do it. Hands at ten and two, like Dad showed me, and keep your eyes on the road. In this case the rutted trail. On the lookout for any fallen trees or rocks, because if we break an axle, the Jeep is all done.

When the trail straightens out, I ask Delphy where she's from.

"Westbrook. We have a Greek restaurant. It's on 302. Delphy's. And no, the restaurant isn't named after me. It's named for my grandmother, Adelphia, who started it."

"Cool."

"It is, mostly. The whole family works there—my mom and dad, aunts and uncles, cousins."

"Sounds like a big place."

She nods. "Started small, but now we seat a hundred and

fifty on Saturday nights. And that's the night I have to scrub pots. Ug!"

I wonder what it must be like, being part of a big family. She makes it sound like fun, even if it does mean scrubbing pots.

We settle in, putting miles between us and the fire.

My passenger gets so relaxed she almost falls asleep, even though the ride is bumpy. With her head lolling and her eyelids drooping, and her faced cleaned of soot, Delphy looks younger. A little girl in a big, tall body. Must be exhausted from her night in the woods. She hasn't really explained what she was doing out there, but she did say she ran her battery down texting someone.

I wonder about that. Why go out in the woods to text? Didn't her camp counselors tell her it's dangerous to be wandering the forests of Maine at night? Didn't they warn about bears and coyotes and bobcats? Or how easy it is to get lost?

After a while, she startles herself awake and goes, "Sorry, sorry. Where are we, Sam?"

"See that little glove compartment? There's a map that might help. Are you good with maps?"

She looks uncertain. "I've got a GPS app. Like that?"

"Never mind. I'll check it out when we stop. Right now, all I know, we're heading mostly west."

"How do you know that?"

I point to the compass on the dash.

"Oh. I was wondering, maybe we can charge my phone from the car battery?"

"I don't think so. It's not like you can just plug in."

She exhales and leans back into her seat, disappointed. "I really, really need my phone. I need to let my parents know what happened. They'll be worried sick. How far before we get to a real road?"

"Don't know. Could be around the next corner. Could be miles."

At exactly that moment, the engine sputters and dies.

The Jeep slows to a stop, dead as a doornail.

12.

Not on This Map

After about a hundred years of totally insane panic—okay, maybe ten seconds—I realize what's wrong and start chuckling. Delphy has this look—like *What have I gotten myself into?*—until I explain that we've run out of gas.

"And why is that funny?"

"Because I can fix it."

I go around to the back, where the two five-gallon fuel cans are strapped to the bumper.

Delphy offers to help. "My ankle hurts but there's nothing wrong with my arms." She grins and makes a muscle.

Turns out she's way stronger than me. Good thing, because the cans are really heavy, and the last thing I want to do is waste gas by spilling it. I unscrew the cap, and we both hold the can as we slowly tip it up, carefully pouring every drop of gas into the empty tank. And then we do it all again with the second can.

"Ten gallons. That should be good for a hundred miles at least."

Delphy's face falls. "You think it's that far, a real road?"

"Hope not. Let's look at the map, see if we can figure it out."

I take the old map out of the glove box and unfold it on the hood. The air is hot and heavy, and although there's no strong smell of smoke, the air is still bad, so breathing is a chore. Sweat is running into my eyes, and I have to blink it away before I can see the map clearly. I'm disappointed it isn't like the trail maps Dad taught me how to read at Baxter State Park. At first it just looks like a bunch of squiggly green lines. The faded printing identifies it as a topographical survey, but I'm not sure what that means, exactly.

Delphy leans over the map, squinting her thoughtful brown eyes, and announces that the lines are marked for elevation.

"Elevation?" I ask.

"How high above sea level, see?"

As soon as she says that, the map suddenly makes sense, like one of those trick puzzles that snap into place once you know the secret. The squiggly green lines trace the shape of land and lakes and mountains. The lines are close together where the mountains are steep, and far apart where the ground is flat, or where there's water.

I lean over the map. "Wabanaski Lake. My camp and your camp are on the same lake, right? If we can find it on the map, at least we'll know where we started."

The printing is tiny, and faded, but we eventually identify the long, skinny shape of the lake. There are no markings for

48

the summer camps located along the shoreline. But the map is old and maybe the camps are more recent, or maybe they just didn't bother marking them down.

Delphy must have really sharp eyes, because she's the one who spots the faint pencil lines. "Could this be the logging road?" she asks.

The pencil markings run east and west across the map, following the lower elevations. The flat land. At one end there's a smudged X, and the other end continues to the far edge of the map.

"Yeah, I think you're right. It makes sense if X is the lumber camp. So we'd be somewhere in here." I place my finger on the smudged pencil line.

"So where does this connect to a main road?"

"It doesn't. Not on this map."

Delphy sighs, her round face concerned. "We're really in trouble, aren't we?"

"Yes. But if we stay ahead of the fire, we'll be okay. That's the main thing: Keep ahead of the fire. It's summer, so we're not going to die of exposure, as long as we have water. And we have food for at least five or six days, if we don't pig out."

Delphy's eyes get even bigger. "For real? You have food?"

I show her the crates in the back seat. Beans, beef stew, franks and beans, Spam, tuna fish. She picks up a can, makes a quirky face. "Are you serious? Bread in a can?"

I nod. "Brown bread. Almost like cake. It's really good, especially with butter. Not that we have any butter."

49

"Huh." She looks over the collection. "Lots of beans."

"Beans are nutritious. Besides, this is Maine. We practically invented baked beans."

For some reason, that makes Delphy laugh. Then she gets serious. "Could you, um, like open a can? I'm starving."

"You choose. I recommend the beef stew."

We don't have spoons, so she sips beef stew right from the can as we drive along the logging trail, keeping a safe distance between us and the fire.

At least for now.

13.

Okay for a Boy

Turns out my passenger is pretty funny when she wants to be. We're bumping along, going maybe ten miles an hour, and suddenly she shades her eyes with her hand and goes, "Slow down! I see the Golden Arches! Big Macs dead ahead!"

For one tiny millisecond I almost fall for it.

"Gotcha!" She grins at me.

"No way."

"Way. You totally believed me."

"You're good," I admit. "Good enough for ice cream. I've been saving the last pint of chocolate chip. In that cooler in the back."

Her eyes dart to the back and I burst out laughing.

She slumps in her seat. "Great. I got away from fatness camp, but I can't get away from imaginary food."

"Fatness camp?"

"They call it fitness because it sounds better. But at least half the girls are there to lose weight."

"Can I ask you a question? Why were you out in the woods at night?"

"No comment." And she won't say any more on the subject.

But here's the thing. After making each other laugh, we're no longer strangers. We're not a team yet, me and Delphy Pappas, but we're getting there.

Late in the day, with light fading through the green leaves, and the smell of smoke ever more distant, we come upon a faded hand-painted sign, nailed to a tree:

PINEY POND COTTAGE
WALK FROM HERE

Delphy says, "If somebody's home, maybe they've got a phone. I really, really want to talk to my mom."

"It's a footpath," I point out. "Too narrow for a vehicle."

But Delphy leverages herself out of the seat, grabs the stick she's using for a crutch, and hobbles past the sign. I'm nervous about leaving the Jeep alone. It saved my life, and my guts tell me to stick with it until we're clear of the forest, clear of the fire. I can't outrun a fire, and for sure Delphy can't. But I need a phone as much as she does, to make sure my mom is okay, and to get us rescued. So I carefully park the Jeep in a cleared space near the sign—this must be where the owners leave their car or truck—and follow her down the footpath.

The path looks like it hasn't been used lately. The undergrowth is so thick with ferns that it's like a wall of soft green waves on either side. Delphy is limping along so fast I can hardly keep up, and I worry she'll trip and make her ankle worse.

"Wait up! Take it easy!" But she's real determined, crashing through the ferns and slashing her stick to clear the path, and then suddenly we're in the clear.

A meadow slopes down to a white cottage on the edge of a small pond. There's a small rickety dock but no boat, and the shutters on the cottage windows are closed.

Nobody home is my guess. But Delphy is determined to find out for sure. A screened-in porch wraps around two sides of the cottage, and she's up the steps and into the porch before I get there. Darting around the old wicker furniture and peering through the glass on the front door, into the dim interior.

She rattles the doorknob. Locked.

"I don't think there's anyone here," I say. "There'd be a car or truck in that spot, right?"

Sounding irritated, she turns to me. "Okay, Sherlock, I get that. Nobody's home! Duh. But what if there's a phone charger in there, or a landline?"

I take a step back. She's taller than me, and holding a big stick. She notices my reaction and her face falls. "Oh, hey. Hey, I'm sorry. I'm just, like, hot and miserable and obsessed about calling my parents, okay?"

"Delphy, I'm pretty sure there aren't any chargers in there."

"How do you know that?"

"Look around. There are no power lines attached to the house. No telephone lines. No lines of any kind."

She hobbles down the steps, looks up at the roofline of the porch and cottage. Her shoulders slump. "This is so messed up."

"There are a lot of places like this in the backwoods. Hunting cabins and getaway cottages that are too remote for power."

"That's stupid."

I shrug, not so sure about that. "It's sort of like camping out, except with a real roof over your head. Summer only, I'm guessing. Unless they come in by snowmobile. That lumber camp? It didn't have power, either."

"I hate this!" Delphy says, frustrated. "Hate it, hate it, hate it!"

"No, no, this is good!" I insist. "This is a great find, even without a phone. We're far enough ahead of the fire that we can hardly smell it. And besides, we don't dare drive a logging trail after dark—too easy to go off the road. So we need a place to stay for the night. The porch is good. The bugs won't be able to chomp on us. Plus, we have chairs and couches and cushions. See? It's way better than sleeping in the Jeep. I'll go back for some food and we'll have a nice supper right here on the porch. How about that?"

Delphy wipes her glistening face with the back of her hand. "You're okay for a boy, you know that?"

14.

Land of a Thousand Dances

On my walk back to the Jeep, I remember something Dad once did with a snowmobile, to make sure it didn't get stolen. He pulled the main spark plug wire and took it with him. *"No spark, no steal,"* he said with a smile.

Doubtful there's anyone around to steal the Jeep, but I can't risk it, not with our lives at stake.

I lift the hood and follow his example.

Thanks, Dad.

When I return with canned goods for supper, Delphy is perched on an old porch rocker, looking very pleased with herself. The door to the cottage is open. "You broke in?"

"Nope." She holds up a key. "Found it under the mat."

The sun is already low in the sky, and the shuttered windows make the inside of the cottage dim. "What's in there?"

Delphy shrugs. "I was waiting for you."

I ease down into a chair. "We're probably breaking the law just being here. Trespassing, right?"

"Said the boy who stole a Jeep."

"Borrowed," I respond quickly.

"Whatever. This is what they call a special circumstance. We're two kids lost in the woods, running from a forest fire, okay? I don't think they'll send us to prison for seeing if there's anything inside that can help us survive."

That makes sense, but it still feels wrong. The pond, the empty dock, the comfortable old porch furniture, it all looks private. Like we're intruding on a family. But Delphy is right—what if there's a phone in there? Or food and water like at the logging camp? "Okay. Let's take a look."

It takes a moment for my eyes to adjust to the deep shadows inside the cabin. Our footsteps echo in a way that makes me think the place is hollow somehow. Then I realize: not hollow, but empty. It even smells empty. There's nothing inside but hot, stale air and an old broom, leaning against a bare wall. No furniture, no pictures on the walls, no wood for the stone fireplace. The cupboard doors are open, and the shelves are bare. No food, water, or supplies. No candles, lanterns, or flashlights. Nothing.

"Whoever they were, the owners, they're gone."

Delphy sighs. "Gone for a long time. Years probably. Look at the dust."

"Sorry."

"It's not your fault." She's being polite, but sounds heartbroken. Delphy pulls open a kitchen drawer, looking for silverware. At first glance, it seems to be as empty as the cupboards, until she reaches to the very back. Then her eyes get bigger.

"I've got something!" she exclaims. "A phone! It's a phone!"

But her excitement doesn't last long. The object from the drawer is about the same size and shape as an old flip phone, but it's not. It's a small, self-powered emergency radio, with a crank on the side. Turn the crank fast for a couple of minutes and the radio will play for a little while.

I take it from her and check it out. "This is really cool, Delphy. My dad had one of these. He used it for the weather reports, when we were hiking. So we'd get warnings of thunderstorms or flash floods. Like that. With the hand crank, you don't have to worry about batteries. Maybe we can find out where the fire is headed!"

Delphy isn't listening. She hobbles out to the porch, keeping her back turned. I know better than to say anything. Plenty of times I've wanted to cry myself, from frustration and fear and not knowing what happens next. Out here in the blazing heat, running from a fire, all you have to do is take a wrong turn, make a bad decision, and you turn into a crispy critter. No second chances once the flames catch up. I can't imagine a worse way to die, but I can't help thinking about it, even though I'm pretty sure we're way ahead of the fire. Anyhow, if Delphy wants to shed a few tears, I'm not going to say a word about it, no way.

I go to the opposite end of the porch and fiddle with the radio, turning the hand crank as fast as I can. After thirty cranks, I switch it on. Static. I rotate the dial. More static.

Behind me, Delphy goes, "Try pulling out the antenna."

Extending the antenna seems to help, but mostly the static is just louder. I give the thing a few more cranks, then fiddle with the dial again, and this time a faint but familiar voice weaves through the static. I turn slowly, aiming the antenna until the voice sharpens. The voice that did our wake-up call, followed by golden oldies. Phat Freddy Bell. Usually he's joking around, but not this time. This time he's dead serious.

"**. . . reporting that more than fifteen thousand acres of dry timberland have been engulfed by wind-driven flames in the last forty-eight hours. In some areas, a wall of flame has spread a mile in less than an hour, leaving nothing but smoldering ash behind. Firefighters are working hard, but they haven't been able to stop it. What started this fire is as yet undetermined. Could be a careless camper, or what they call 'dry lightning.' But whatever started it, officials fear this may be worse than the great fire of 1947 that burned from the mountains to the sea, destroying town after town. Unless we get some rain. Boy, do we need rain. So we're praying for rain! We're dancing for rain! That's right, your host Phat Freddy Bell is dancin' right now in the 'RPZ studio, making a fool of himself. Come on, come on! Let's all get up and dance! Old and young! Everybody! Dance until it rains!**"

The voice blends into music, wild rocking music about the land of a thousand dances, but it quickly fades to static.

Delphy tucks the radio into her backpack, then looks at me with worried eyes. "We're in bad trouble."

15.

The Fart Heard Round the World

We're sitting on the screen porch in the dark, both of us groaning because our stomachs are so full. Cold beans and franks may not sound appetizing, but it is if you're starving. And the beans weren't really cold, not in this heat. Must be ninety degrees with the sun down. To top it off, we each ate a can of brown bread, and even without butter it was delicious.

Delphy, contented, says, "This is the fullest I've been since before Camp Fatness, and all those so-called healthy meals. It feels good not to be hungry."

"I don't know about the other campers, but you're not, you know, fat or anything. You're tall for a girl, that's all. Tall and big and strong. But definitely not, um, overweight."

"Ha. Tall and big and strong. Just what every girl wants to hear."

"I'm serious."

"Let's talk about something else." She leans back in her porch rocker and massages her sore ankle.

It's so dark the world outside the porch might as well be a pool of black ink. No stars, and the smell of smoke remains faint and distant, which means we don't have to worry about the fire. Not right this minute, anyhow.

Delphy clears her throat. "Know what I want more than anything? A hot shower to wash my hair. I smell like a dirt-ball and everything feels gross, like I've been dipped in grease, then rolled around in the dirt. Ugh!"

"No plumbing in this cabin, but tomorrow morning, first light, we can wash up in the pond."

"That would be cool. So what do *you* want more than anything?"

No need to think about it. "Call my mom."

Her expression softens. "What would you tell her?"

"That I'm okay and not to worry."

Delphy nods. "I wish it was true, that there's nothing to worry about. How far away are we from the fire?"

"Miles. I hope."

"That DJ on the radio said it was spreading a mile an hour. So every time we stop moving, it might be catching up. Right?"

I shake my head, because I know what's she's about to ask. "No way. We can't drive at night. Not on that trail. We'd wreck the Jeep and then we'd be toast."

"No, no. Totally. I get it."

"Unless you think *you* can drive at night, on a trail we don't know."

60

"Hey, Sam? I can't drive at all, okay? No clue. I'm not, like, being critical or anything. I'm just worried." She sighs. "So if the fire does catch up, can't we just jump in the pond?"

I think about it. "Maybe. If that's our only option. It's risky. Our camp counselor told us it's better to find another way out, if possible. Even in a pond, if you're not far enough away from the burning shoreline, the smoke from a big fire might make it too hard to breathe. It depends on if we want to burn to death, or die from smoke inhalation."

"Great choice."

"Don't worry, Delphy. The fire can't catch us, not as long as we have the Jeep."

"Thanks, Sam. What do we do next?"

"Before the lumber camp burned, I had a plan. I was going to chop down some birch saplings and make a big 'HELP' sign that could be seen from the air."

She perks up. "That's a great idea. Except I haven't heard any search planes overhead, have you? Or helicopters?"

"No. But somebody has to be looking for us. Right?"

"Unless they think we're dead."

"There are a bunch of camps on Lake Wabanaski. Your camp and my camp, and the YMCA on the far side of the lake. Plus lots of summer cottages. What I mean is, the fire came up so fast we can't be the only ones missing."

"True. I'll help you make the sign if you think it might work."

"Awesome."

We sit there in the dark for a while, not saying anything. At first it feels awkward, and then I kind of relax into the silence. People don't have to talk every second. They can just be quiet together. Not perfectly quiet, though, because my stomach is rumbling, which is embarrassing. Not that Delphy says anything about it.

To cover up the rumble, I ask if she has any brothers or sisters.

She nods. "Angie and Calista. Five years younger. They're twins. Not identical, but they might as well be. They had their own language until they were like six years old. They still call me the BFG, or Geegee for short."

"BFG?"

"Big Friendly Giant." She laughs. "They love that book so much I guess I should be flattered. What about you?"

"It's just me and Mom." I leave it at that. "Did your parents make you go to camp? Is that why you wanted to run away?"

She jerks back, offended. "Who says I was running away? I got lost in the woods, that's all."

"Okay. Sorry."

Not something she wants to discuss, obviously.

"It was my dad's idea, to try a fitness camp," she continues. "Especially the volleyball program. He wants me to 'use my tall.' Turns out I like track better, but volleyball is okay."

"Use your tall?"

"Like embrace it. Dad is six foot five. He thinks it's cool, having a tall daughter. Says he wants me to have altitude instead of attitude."

"Sounds like a cool guy."

"My dad? He wouldn't know cool if it bit him on the butt."

That makes me chuckle. "You're pretty funny, you know that?"

"So now I'm big and tall and funny. That's just great."

I sigh. "I'm never going to beat you, am I?"

"Never, ever, ever. Accept that, little man."

"Hey!"

"Accept that, average-heighted-boy-for-his-age."

Even in the dark I can tell she's grinning. She likes it, us bouncing stuff off each other, making wisecracks. I never had a big sister, but maybe this is what it's like.

"I've got a plan," she says. "You know what my plan is? My plan is, tomorrow we get rescued."

"Great. That's my plan, too."

And then it happens. Without warning, or any way to stop it, I let one rip. I mean *really* rip. It sounds like an out-of-control whoopee cushion, venting loud and long. Like a not-so-distant artillery barrage. Like—oh, never mind, you know what it sounds like.

When at long last it's over, I gasp and say the first thing that comes to mind. "Beans."

That does it. Delphy goes bonkers, and then I'm laughing, too, and it's like contagious or something. We can't stop, we keep laughing and giggling until we're out of breath. And then Delphy snickers and shouts, "Beans!" and we start laughing all over again. Laughing until my stomach hurts so bad I have to jam my fist in my mouth to stop the giggles.

"Beans, beans, the musical fruit," she chants.

"Stop!" I beg her. "Don't."

"The more you eat, the more you toot!"

I never knew that you can laugh yourself to sleep, but you can, under the right circumstances.

Day Three

16.

The Sound of Engines

In my dream an angry wasp is buzzing around my head, but for some reason my hands don't work, they're too heavy to lift, so I can't stop the wasp. What if it gets in my ear? What if it stings my brain?

That's what wakes me up, fear of a stung brain. I'm lying on the porch with a cushion for a pillow. There's some light in the sky, but not much. A little after dawn, is my guess. The air feels super hot and syrup thick. Gusts of wind rattle the trees.

I sit up, feeling sore from the hard porch floor, and look around. Delphy is slumped in the rocker, still sound asleep. I stand up carefully, not wanting to wake her, and search for the wasp buzzing against the screens. Because I didn't dream that part, there really is an insect noise.

No, wait, not an insect. A distant engine, like a chain saw, or maybe a dirt bike. It fades in and out with the wind, but there is more than one engine. Two at least.

My heart starts slamming. People! They're finally coming to rescue us, cutting a path through the woods.

I shake Delphy. She lurches awake, and not happily. "Hey, what are you doing? Leave me alone."

"Listen! Can you hear that?"

She grabs her stick and gets to her feet, wincing from the pain in her swollen ankle. I help her down from the porch and we make our way through the meadow, down toward the pond. Toward the sound of gunning engines.

As we get closer to the pond, we see flashes on the opposite shore. Not a light, but fast-moving shapes.

Then I notice what we missed last evening in the fading sunset. Part of a roof and chimney, visible through the trees swaying in the wind. There's a good-sized summer house on the opposite shore, and the shapes that are moving fast are a couple of dirt bikes zooming around the property. Above the noise of the revving engines, we can hear the riders whooping it up, shouting, "Away! Away!" or something like it. Hard to tell, exactly.

"We should yell back." Delphy drops her stick and waves her arms.

"Wait. Not yet."

I've got a bad feeling about the wild riders. Why are they circling the house and whooping it up? What are they celebrating? Are they having a party?

Delphy, ignoring my cautions, shouts, "Hey! Hey! Over here! Across the pond! Help! Help! Help!"

The bikes keep zooming around the house, vanishing

into the trees and then reappearing. Maybe they can't hear her above the scream of their engines.

What happens next makes my blood run cold. An orange light comes on inside the house, making a window glint. The light grows quickly, filling the house, getting brighter and brighter, and then it bursts through the roof as orange flames, leaping into the sky, lighting up the tall pine trees.

Fire, exploding from the house and spreading fast, driven by the wind.

"Delphy! We have to get out of here! They saw us for sure!"

She's staring at the fire, as if she can't believe it. Her hope of rescue going up in flames.

Across the pond, one of the dirt-bike riders comes to the edge of the water, looking directly at us. He raises his arm and points wildly. The other rider suddenly roars up beside him. Then they zoom off, vanishing into the woods ahead of the fire.

Do they know about the Jeep? Maybe spotted it from the logging trail as they zoomed around the pond to have their fun? No time to think about it. Concentrate on getting away from the fire.

The fire. The fire.

The fire grows like a thing alive, doubling every few seconds, getting hotter and brighter, until the whole pond glows orange and red, like there's a fire inside the pond. A wave of intense heat scorches the air. Black smoke spreads across the pond like night fog, but way more deadly. Fog you can breathe, but not hot smoke.

The weird thing is, it's so beautiful you can't stop watching it.

"Delphy!"

She turns to me, blinking her eyes as if she's just woken up from a dream.

"We have to go! They might be trying to find us! They might have seen the Jeep!"

"They're the ones," she says. "They started the whole thing."

"Probably. Come on!"

She grabs hold of my shoulder and uses her stick for balance. We limp-run up the meadow, away from the pond, away from the fire. Delphy insists on retrieving her backpack, and I keep urging her to hurry.

We have to get to the Jeep before the dirt-bike riders find us.

I don't know how I know they're coming for us, but I do.

17.

Burning the World

By the time we get to the Jeep, the searing hot wind has thickened with smoke. Our eyes are watering from a crummy combination of sweat, smoke, and tears. I help Delphy into the passenger seat, toss her backpack into the rear seat, and then leap behind the wheel. Hoping with all my heart that the engine will start when I flip the lever and depress the starting pedal.

It turns over but doesn't catch. My heart sinks. And then I remember the secret to making it start is in my pocket.

"What's wrong?" Delphy asks.

No time to explain. I race to the front, lift the hood, and plug the wire into the distributor cap.

Back behind the wheel, I close my eyes and flip the starter switch.

Vrrrroooom. What a beautiful sound!

"Hang on!" I shout, and let out the clutch.

A moment later, we're barreling along the old logging trail with the hot wind at our backs. Which isn't good, because it means the wind is pushing the fire and smoke in our direction.

But going the other way would have taken us back into the fire, so this is our only option.

I'm gripping the wheel with all my might as we bounce along the ruts. Concentrating on keeping the vehicle on the trail and not veering off or colliding with a stump. The thing is, with my eyes watering, I'm not seeing all that good.

"Look behind!" I shout to Delphy. "Is it catching up?"

"I don't know! Maybe! The whole sky is on fire!"

I press down on the accelerator until the pedal hits the floor. We're flying, hitting twenty miles an hour according to the speed gauge. There's only one way to make it go faster, and that's to change gears. Which is something I haven't attempted at full speed, because until now second gear was fast enough.

"Hang on!"

I push in the clutch, push the gear lever down and to the right, and let the clutch out. Third gear!

Much faster. Too fast, the way we're being rattled around, so I let up slightly on the gas pedal. Thirty-five miles an hour. On a highway, that would be slow as a snail. On an uneven, unpaved logging road, it feels like a hundred miles an hour. And it's working. The smoke is thinning, and that means we're outrunning the fire. Which doesn't make my heart pound any less. We need to get far away. Miles and miles. Back at the pond, the fire moved like a sprinter, racing from a cottage roof to a full-blown wildfire in minutes. Everything so dry, just waiting to explode into flame. And those dirt bikers racing around like gleeful devils, chanting, "Away! Away!" and burning the world.

Did I hear them wrong? Was that really what they were shouting? And why does it sound so familiar?

One thing I know for sure, the bikers spotted us from across the pond. Me and Delphy are witnesses to a crime. Does that mean they'll try to run us down? Shut us up?

Maybe the fire scares them more than we do. If it was me, I'd want to have the wind in my face, pushing the flames in the opposite direction. Fastest way to get clear and safe. And besides, we weren't close enough to see their faces, let alone identify them.

That's what I keep telling myself as we slam along the ruts, teeth rattling. If we get far away from the fire, we'll also be far away from the dirt bikers.

With the Jeep going this fast, Delphy has to yell to make herself heard. "I need to use the ladies' room!"

I slow down and put the gearshift in neutral and let us roll to a stop. No way am I going to shut off the engine, not when something might be catching up. Fire or bad guys or both.

Of course, there's no ladies' room, so Delphy takes a small roll of TP from her backpack, limps to a row of bushes, and disappears behind them. There's no smoke showing under the canopy of trees, just plain gray sky. And now that we're stopped, I notice the wind is no longer blowing in our direction. It's barely blowing at all, and seems to have shifted. All good.

I strain to listen for the chain-saw sound of dirt bikes, but can't hear anything.

Delphy comes limping back and heaves herself into the passenger seat. "Sorry."

"It's okay. The radio is in your backpack, right? Maybe we can get an update on the fire."

I crank the little radio as fast as possible. Then turn it on and slowly pan the antenna around until it catches the signal.

"**. . . Fire Service officials announced that the fight to contain the fire will concentrate resources and personnel on the southeastern edges of the conflagration. That's a big word for 'fire,' but it's fun to say. Con-flah-gray-shun! They explained that the northern areas are thinly populated, whereas in the south, six to a dozen towns and villages are under threat. So, Bigfoot, if you're out there, you better get runnin', because nobody is coming to help! Just kidding, rock 'n' rollers. I'm raising my mug of morning coffee in a toast to our brave firefighters, who are risking their lives to contain this awful blaze. Good luck! Be safe! This is Phat Freddy Bell, high atop the lowest official mountain in the great state of Maine . . .**"

When the music comes back on, I switch it off.

"They're concentrating on the south," Delphy says, in a croaky kind of whisper. "We're in the north."

I nod.

"So we're on our own. Totally."

"Looks like it." I try to sound upbeat. "But we have been all along, and we're doing okay. We're still alive, right?"

Delphy sighs. "Any idea where we're going?"

"Mostly west." I point at the compass on the dashboard.

"What about the map?"

"I'm pretty sure we're off the map by now."

"What do we do?"

I shrug. "Keep driving until we bump into a real road. Or a fire crew. Or somebody."

"But not them!" Delphy shudders. "Not those creeps!"

"Not them," I agree.

"I can't believe I waved at those jerks."

"Doesn't matter now. We're making good progress."

I get the Jeep back up to third gear and keep going for what must be a solid hour. Chalking up the miles. Figuring maybe eighty more miles in the tank before we run out of gas.

Not sure how far away from the fire we've gotten, because the old logging road meanders around, looking for a level pathway through the deep woods. Deep and getting deeper. The spruces and pines are much taller here, towering into the gray sky, blocking sunlight. Kind of spooky, really, like if you turned your back, the giant trees might come alive. Of course, they *are* alive, but you know what I mean.

I'm thinking about how I'll describe all this to Mom, how I'll make it a really good story, when we come around a corner and everything changes.

Standing tall in the pathway is a great big moose. A big bull moose with antlers like radar scoops, and he's not about to move.

I jam on the brakes. We start to skid, turning sideways as I fight for control. The wheels hit the ruts the wrong way, and suddenly we're flying through the air.

18.

It's a Girl Thing

By rights we should be dead. In a forest full of sharp branches and big rocks, we're somehow flung into a thick patch of soft ferns. I land on my back, hard enough to knock the breath out of me. I turn over onto my hands and knees, gasping for air. Ten feet away, deep in the ferns, I see Delphy with her big eyes wide open, staring in amazed confusion.

"What happened?" she asks.

"Moose" is all I can manage to say.

"I mean to your Jeep! I thought it was going to land on top of us."

I crawl out of the ferns, onto the logging road, and can't believe my eyes. The Jeep is up on its side, undercarriage exposed, leaning against a tree, one tire still spinning. Delphy's right—if the tree hadn't been there to block it, the vehicle might have killed us both.

The moose is gone, vanished back into the woods.

Delphy limps over, puts a hand on my shoulder. "I'm so sorry. I know that Jeep was like your friend or something."

I don't know what to say. If we don't have the Jeep, how are we going to escape the fire? How are we going to find our way back to civilization? It's not like firefighters are on their way to save us.

Delphy cautiously approaches the Jeep. "You think it's totaled?" she asks.

"I don't know." I feel helpless.

Glass from the shattered headlights and the smashed windshield is scattered across the ground. Other than that, the Jeep looks more or less in one piece, except it's leaning up against a tree.

Canned goods and water jugs have been thrown in the underbrush. I gather them up while I try to figure out what happens next.

Meanwhile, Delphy finds herself a new walking stick, and then snags her backpack from the leaning Jeep. She perches on an old stump and starts winding the charger on the radio, then aims the antenna around, honing in on the signal, which is stronger than it was the last time.

"... your WRPZ host Phat Freddy Bell, high atop the lowest official mountain in the great state of Maine. Wish I had better news, but the fact is it's getting worse. In the early morning hours, wildfire erupted in the vicinity of remotely situated Piney Pond, and quickly engulfed hundreds of acres, cutting off power to this corner of the county. We're on backup generator now, with enough fuel for a few days. Heck, I'll siphon the gas out of my car, if it comes to that.

I'm planning on sticking it out, and making these reports in the hope it will help. If there's anybody listening! Phone lines are down, too, so I can't be sure of that. But if you are listening, here's something you need to know.

"Satellite images indicate that the Piney Pond fire was probably arson. Hard to believe there's someone out there angry enough, or evil enough, or stupid enough, to deliberately start a fire in a tinder-dry forest. But what do I know? I'll tell you this much: It's getting personal. I can see fire and smoke from the studio window. Miles away but moving in this direction. And you know the weird thing? I never thought of a fire as being alive, but it sure looks like it's living and breathing, except it's breathing flames instead of air. Whew! Forecast says there's a chance of thunderstorms later in the day. Sure hope they're right, because, boy oh boy, do we need rain!"

The sound fades out, turning to static, and Delphy stares at the little radio. "I can't believe it. We were there, Sam! We were right there watching when those two creeps started the fire. Hundreds of acres. Out of control. And nobody knows who did it but us."

"We don't know who did it. Not really. Except they were guys on dirt bikes."

"Young guys with long faces and blond beards. Tattoos on their arms."

"Are you serious? All I saw was the bikes. You must have eyes like an eagle."

79

"You noticed the bikes, I noticed the boys." She smiles. "It's a girl thing."

I make a pile of the canned goods, sorting them for nourishment. There's only so many we can carry if we're on foot, and we'll have to make them count.

"What's the plan?" Delphy wants to know, limping over to inspect the cans.

"We have to keep moving. If those dirt bikers come this way, we're toast. Same for the fire."

"Do what you have to, but I'm not walking." She's defiant. "See this swollen ankle? The more I walk, the worse it gets. There's only one thing to do, one thing that makes sense."

"What's that?"

"Fix the stupid Jeep."

"How?"

Her grin gets bigger. "We do what the Greeks do."

19.

Sort of Lost

"My grandfather was born in Greece and came here as a kid," Delphy explains. "He loves this country and everything, but he's also super proud of being Greek. Thousands of years ago, Greeks invented a lot of important stuff that we still use today. Anyway, my *pappou* is a stonemason, and he talks a lot about this ancient Greek named Archimedes, who claimed he could move the world if he had a big enough lever. Because that's what Pappou does—he moves big stones and rocks with levers and crowbars. He's a little dude, my grandfather, shorter and smaller than me, but he can shift a two-thousand-pound stone easy peasy. Trust me, tipping this Jeep back on the level would be a piece of cake for him."

"Too bad he's not here." I'm not sure where she's going with this.

"Oh, he is." Delphy taps her skull. "Right here. I've been helping Pappou since I was little. If I'm strong, that's why."

Despite what she said about her sore ankle, it doesn't slow her down much. Next thing you know, she's dragging me into the woods to find fallen branches we can use as levers. It blows my mind that she's so confident that we can do it, rescue the poor Jeep. "The best thing, we've got the tree as the fulcrum. Some call it the pivot point. I can't do the math—Archimedes is the one who came up with the formula—but instinct tells me we need a lever at least ten feet long and strong enough so it won't break. But not so heavy we can't lift it!"

Sweaty and hot, we work our way through the underbrush. Most of the fallen branches we find are rotten and useless. Delphy says hardwoods would be the best, like oak. But this particular stretch of forest is mostly pine and spruce, so we're stuck with that.

As we search, I keep my eye on the logging road. Don't dare stray too far, or we're likely to get lost. And that makes me think about my dad, and how much he loved hiking, and being outdoors. Probably all those twelve-hour days in a truck cab made him crave fresh air. Anyhow, I'm sort of lost in my own thoughts as we kick our way through the underbrush. I'm not really paying attention when Delphy stops and looks up, squinting into the dense coverage overhead.

"Hear that?" She inhales sharply. "Is that what I think it is?"

It's a plane. Unmistakable. A prop plane. And getting closer.

"We need to find a clearing! They'll never see us through these trees!"

And then we're running, or trying to run, because it's hard in the underbrush with so many things underfoot. The miserable heat makes it even harder. Delphy's swinging along with her walking stick tucked under her arm like a crutch. "Come on, come on! Find us! Please, please, please!"

I've got no choice but to follow, and anyhow she's right: To be seen from the air, we have to find a clearing in the forest. I want to get rescued as bad as she does. So we're running deeper into the woods, following the tantalizing drone of the plane. Hoping to find an opening in the forest canopy. Hoping to be seen. Hoping to be rescued.

Hoping, hoping, hoping.

"Got to see us! Got to see us! Got to see us!" Delphy chants to herself as she limp-runs.

It's all I can do to keep up. I don't know about her, but I'm in full panic mode. Heart revving like a race-car engine, head pounding with excitement, sweat pouring into my eyes. A plane! A chance to be rescued! Hot showers and hot meals! A phone call to Mom! Better yet, I'll just show up, make sure she's okay. What a surprise that will be—she probably thinks I'm dead. By now they'll have told her what happened at camp. The wildfire evacuation and me missing the bus. Maybe she checked herself out of rehab to join the search! Assuming there *is* a search. Can't blame them for thinking I probably got killed in the fire.

Whatever, I need to let Mom know I'm alive. Because I can't imagine what she'll do if she thinks both me and Dad are gone forever. Go back on the pills, or worse. And worse I can't bear thinking about, even though I do think about it all the time, of course I do.

More than anything I want a happy ending.

I mean, life was so tough and miserable that first year after Dad died, and Mom tried so hard to keep us going, just me and her. Us against the world. One for all and all for one. We deserve a happy ending, just this once.

Please, please, please.

We never do find a clearing. Not that we ever see the plane, the canopy is so thick. But the sound of the prop engines gets fainter and fainter, and then they disappear. Silence, except for Delphy leaning against a tree, sobbing in frustration.

"This is *so* unfair."

"Yeah, it is. It really is."

Delphy rubs her eyes and looks around. "Where's the Jeep?" she wants to know. "What direction?"

"We weren't exactly running in a straight line," I tell her cautiously, not wanting to upset her more than she's already upset.

"What are you saying?"

I take a deep breath. "We're sort of, um, ah . . ."

"'Um ah' what?" she demands.

"Lost," I say, with a great sinking feeling. "We're lost in the woods."

20.

Totally Boogered

The most important thing when you're lost is not to panic. Running around like a chicken with your head cut off will only make matters worse. Once you realize you're lost, you have to stop and make a plan.

Making a plan and sticking to it kept me alive that first day when I missed the bus, and it can help now.

First thing, try and determine which way is north. If the sun is low in the sky and you know it's afternoon, then put the sun on your left-hand side and you'll be facing north. If the sky is overcast or dark, or you just can't tell where the sun is, check the moss on the trees. Chances are most of the moss will be concentrated on the north side of the tree trunk.

"How do you know all this?" Delphy sounds amazed. "Are you a Boy Scout?"

"My dad. He loved to hike and camp and stuff."

"That's great, but how does knowing which way is north help if we don't know where we are?"

"It's a place to start. First we establish north, then we walk east or west, blazing a trail."

Delphy looks at me with something like astonishment. "Blazing a trail. Whatever that is."

"It's a way to keep us going. Making sure we don't circle back on ourselves. In the deep woods, you think you're walking a straight line, but chances are you're going around in a circle. Dad explained it to me. Your dominant foot strides slightly longer, okay? Makes you veer to the right or left. One way to be sure you're going straight is to leave marks as you go, like a cut in the tree bark. If you circle back, you'll know. That's what trailblazing is—the blaze is the mark on the tree."

Delphy nods thoughtfully. "I guess that makes sense. Um, speaking of circles, did you notice the plane wasn't circling?"

My heart sinks. "It wasn't, was it? It sort of just kept going."

"If it was a search plane, it would have been circling, right?"

"I guess."

"So it just happened to pass overhead. Heading for the fire, maybe. Not looking for us." Delphy sounds discouraged. "We have to find your Jeep, or we're totally boogered."

"Totally boogered," I echo.

"Do you think they'll find our burned-up bodies, or will we melt into the ash?"

"Hey! We're not going to burn up, that's a promise."

She makes a face. "You don't know that."

"I can't explain it, but I'm a thousand percent sure we're going to be okay."

She snorts. "Based on what?"

"Based on the fact we're not going to give up."

"Who said I was going to give up?" She's indignant. "I'm just mad about getting us lost. I'm not giving up, you got that straight?"

"You didn't get us lost. We both got us lost."

"Whatever. So, you figured out which way is north?"

I nod and point.

She adjusts her walking stick, tucking it firmly under her arm. "Then we better start—what did you call it?—blazing a trail. The sunlight is already fading, and I have no intention—none whatsoever—of spending a night in the woods. I don't care if my ankle swells up to the size of a basketball, we're not stopping till we find the Jeep."

In the old days, they left the blaze mark on the trees with an ax or a hatchet. We don't have an ax or a hatchet, and trying to carve a mark with the jackknife would take too long. Another way is to mark each tree with a strip of cloth, and that gives me an idea.

"Delphy, what happened to your backpack?"

"Left it by that tree stump near the Jeep. Why?"

Discouraged, I explain about using strips of cloth for markers.

She gets a funny look in her eye. "Maybe I can help with that."

Turns out she's wearing a swimsuit under her clothes, from that first night she spent in the woods. Whoever was supposed to meet her, they had planned on swimming in the moonlight. "I didn't want him to think I'd go skinny-dipping, so I wore a one-piece." She sounds ticked off, so I keep my trap shut. "Stay where you are, Sam. Be right back."

She emerges from behind a thick patch of tall ferns with a lifeguard-red swimsuit over her arm.

I cut it into strips with my jackknife. It takes a while. Delphy looks on with a sour expression. I don't think ruining the swimsuit is what bothers her. More like being reminded that her friend never showed up. Whatever, she takes a handful of the bright red strips and helps me mark the trees as we hike through the dense woods. It's hot, miserable work.

My gut tells me the logging trail is to the east, and I'm pretty sure that's the way we're heading. We tramp maybe a mile through the dimming forest, dry pine needles crunching under our feet, making sure we're never out of sight of the last tree marked. Trying to keep in as straight a line as possible.

Nothing. No logging trail, just more trees. So much for my stupid gut.

"It's going to be dark in a few minutes." Delphy's voice is full of dread.

"Double darn rat puke."

She laughs. "Is that the best you can do?"

"I pledged not to swear."

"You really are a Boy Scout," she says with something like affection. "Good for you, and lucky for me. Okay, so what do we do next?"

It's not like we have a lot of choices. Before the last of the light fails, we pick out a nice big tree and sit with our backs against the trunk. The ground is uncomfortable and the tree is rough against our shoulders. The only good thing, there's no danger of getting a chill. Plus, being with another person somehow makes me less afraid of bears.

Not that I mention the word "bear," because there's no reason to give Delphy something else to worry about.

"I wonder how much blood you lose in each mosquito bite?" she asks. "I must be down a pint by now."

"Mosquitoes suck, they really do."

"Ha ha."

"It could be worse."

"Oh really? How?"

"We could be alone."

"We *are* alone, dummy."

"No. I mean alone alone. Then you'd get bitten twice as much."

She chuckles. "You're funny. Do you think you can sleep, leaning against this tree?"

"No way."

"Me neither."

We sit in silence for a while, leaning against the hard bark of the tree. Me personally, I'm wishing for a nice cool pillow.

That and wondering what Mom is doing at this very instant. Hoping she's not alone. She had friends before the pills got in the way. But true friends would keep her company in an emergency, wouldn't they?

I'm not sure, and that makes me sad and worried.

Delphy breaks the silence. "Can I ask you a question, Sam? It's like really personal."

"Okay."

"What happened to your father? You don't have to answer if you don't want to."

I shrug. "He's dead."

"I figured that. But how did he die?"

So I tell her.

21.

Secrets Sad but True

No need to gross Delphy out with the gruesome details, so I give her the general idea. That Dad was a civilian truck driver in Afghanistan, making really good money, and there was an accident and he didn't survive. I don't mention what kind of tanker he was driving, or exactly how he was killed, because I can barely stand to think of it myself, even though it's always there in the back of my head.

It's kind of amazing I can talk about my dead father without freaking out, but after three years, it's my reality. A terrible thing happened, and no matter how much you ache to have him back, it can't be changed. That first year was the worst, with some days worse than others, like his birthday and every holiday and Sunday nights and especially Christmas. Me and Mom went to grief counseling, and that helped a little, but it never goes away. You just have to live with it, and one thing I know for sure, Dad wouldn't want us to be sad forever, not all the time. No way. He loved us way too much.

After I finish, Delphy doesn't say anything for a long time, and then she goes, "Hey, Sam? I got lucky when you drove by. You saved my life, so thanks. And I'm sorry for thinking you were some little dork showing off with a stolen Jeep. You're an amazing person and your father would be so proud."

"Huh! I don't know about that. My dad thought letting yourself get lost in the woods was really lame."

"That was an accident," she says earnestly. "An accident, okay? We got excited by the plane. It would have happened to anybody."

"We'll find the trail, Delphy, as soon as the sun comes up. How's your ankle?"

"Fine. Sort of. It only hurts when I put weight on it."

We sit quietly together, propped up against the scratchy tree. Not talking about the fire, or how it might catch up, but it's always there in the back of my mind. It's full dark now— I can barely make out my hand in front of my face—and night noises are starting. A brittle creaking from the tall trees as they react to the warm wind. A fluttering of wings— birds taking shelter in the pine and spruce branches, or so I hope. Something light and furtive padding over the pine needles. What lives in these woods?

Best not to think about it. Best to cover the mysterious noises with the sound of our voices. Maybe that will scare the critters away.

I say, "Can I ask *you* a personal question? What were you really doing out in the woods in the first place, if you were going swimming?"

"That was dumb, huh? Can you keep a secret?"

"I swear."

"Okay." She sighs. "I was supposed to meet this guy, Jason Dean? He's a counselor at your camp. We've been texting. Just plain texting, nothing bad. We never met in person, and my two weeks were almost over, so finally he texted for us to meet up on this trail behind my camp, after lights-out, and we'd go to a good spot he knew on the lake."

"And he never showed?"

She laughs, but not a funny laugh. An angry, hurt kind of laugh. "What was I thinking? That a super-cute guy like Jason would actually want to meet me? In his first text, he said he had his eye on me. As if. What a joke. And there I was with a swimsuit and a beach towel. Pathetic."

"I'm sorry."

"The really stupid thing? I waited until after midnight, because he kept texting he'd be there any minute. That went on for hours! I bet they were laughing themselves sick, him and his friends. Pranking this pathetic loser girl."

"You're not a loser."

She says, scornfully, "No? Big and tall might be okay for some girls, but me? You think I don't know what I look like? Big Friendly Giant, ho ho ho!"

"Delphy, stop." There's nothing worse than when someone's hurting and you can't do anything about it.

She takes a deep, shuddering breath. "Let's get one thing straight. I'm not crying because of Jason Dean. I'm crying

93

because mosquitoes are eating me alive and I'm thirsty and hot and hungry and tired and wish I was anywhere but here." She pauses. "No offense."

"None taken."

"Are there bears in these woods? Tell the truth."

"Not in this part of the forest," I lie.

Bears aren't the only lie. Because I know for a fact there's no counselor named Jason Dean at Camp Wabanaski. Whatever rotten person pranked Delphy, he was too cowardly to use his own name.

Day Four

22.

Not Bad for Wonder Woman

I wake up coughing. Smoke in the air. I leap to my feet and stare at the early morning sky above the swaying treetops. That familiar ash-gray tint means there's a fire burning somewhere nearby, too close for comfort.

"Delphy! Wake up!"

Her face is so puffy and swollen by bug bites I almost don't recognize her. From her reaction, I must look the same, or worse.

"Fire coming! We have to find the logging trail fast!"

Delphy pushes herself upright, props the walking stick under her arm. "Let's go. What direction?"

"East didn't work. Let's try south."

Deciding which way is south takes longer than I expect, with my head still full of sleep and bad dreams, but finally we set off. As usual, I have trouble keeping up with Delphy, who only has one good leg. Girl could circle the world and I'd still be tying my shoes. We don't bother to blaze the trees, there's no time for that. We just have to try our best to move in a straight line.

We keep the wind behind us, and that helps. My heart is racing and my brain is all jumbled, but there's one thing I know for sure: If we don't find the logging trail and the Jeep, we're in big, big trouble. I've seen how fast wind-driven wild-fires can move, eating up the landscape, turning everything into flame.

We can't see the fire, but I know it's there, somewhere behind us. Might still be a few miles away. Maybe we have time to get ahead of it. But not without the Jeep. Fast as we're going, we can't outrun fire. We need wheels, and speed, not to mention luck.

I'm glancing behind us, checking on how straight we're going, when Delphy cries out. "Sam! Over there!"

At first I think she means the fire, and I almost don't dare to look where she's pointing. Not straight ahead, but off to the side. A gap in the trees, brightened by daylight.

We race to the daylight and find ourselves on the old rutted logging trail! "Oh, Delphy, you did it! You found it!" I throw my arms around her. "You did it!"

She shoves me away with a grimace of pain. "You're standing on my foot."

"Sorry."

"Which way, Sam?" she asks. "Two choices!"

The urgency in her voice hits me like a slap of cold water. She's right. Finding the logging trail is great, it's amazing, but we still have to locate the Jeep.

Two choices, right or left.

I nod at her. "You pick."

Immediately she swings her bad foot to the right and starts loping along. I have to jog to keep up. "This looks familiar," I say, panting. "See? That's our tire track. Has to be! Which means we came this way, and the Jeep must be somewhere ahead."

"Hurry!" She picks up the pace.

Is it my imagination or has the smoke thickened? Is the fire getting closer? Is the air harder to breathe, or do my lungs hurt because I'm jogging in this awful, endless heat?

Freaking out doesn't help, I tell myself. Concentrate on the task at hand. *Find the Jeep.* Then you can worry about levering it off the tree, and getting away from the fire, and whatever else happens next.

Taking things one at a time makes sense, and it sounds easy, but my mind is swirling with a thousand thoughts and concerns. Escaping the fire, sure, but worrying about Mom is right up there. At best she knows I'm missing; at worst she thinks I'm dead. Is she sticking with the program, or has worrying about me set her back on the wrong path? How long has it been since the fire started? It feels like a week, but it can't be that long. Night at the logging camp is one. Cottage by the pond is two. Night lost in the woods is three.

Three nights, four days. How long before the fire burns itself out, or gets contained by firefighters? A week? It can't be as long as a month, can it? Because we'll never make it that long. We'll run out of food and water. We'll run out of gasoline, and out of luck.

Stop thinking about stuff you can't control! Concentrate on the task at hand, which is keeping up with Delphy. Who lopes furiously along, crutch-stick pounding into the dirt, her face a puffy mask of determination.

Ignore the smoky taste in your mouth and the ache in your lungs, and follow that girl.

Ahead of us the logging trail takes a curve to avoid a huge, lichen-covered rock. Which rings a bell in my exhausted brain. I remember seeing that big rock out of the corner of my eye just before the moose appeared. Sure enough, there it is— the Jeep! It's still leaning up against the tree, exactly as we left it when we started chasing after the plane.

Delphy limps up and whacks the vehicle with her walking stick. "Yes!" She turns to me with an expression of triumph. "Not bad for a girl with a limp, eh?"

We slap five. "Are you kidding? Not bad for Wonder Woman!"

23.

Hot Snowflakes

"What's that?" Delphy wants to know, looking up at a patch of sky.

We're searching along the logging trail for a branch that's strong enough to pry the Jeep off the tree. Making sure we don't stray out of sight of the trail—one night lost in the woods is more than enough, thank you—when Delphy notices something in the air.

It looks like gray snowflakes.

"Ash." I hold out my hand to catch a few flakes. "Still warm. Blowing ahead of the fire, I guess."

"We don't have much time, do we?"

"I don't know. Honest. Phat Freddy said it was moving a mile an hour. But that was yesterday. With this wind, who knows?"

Delphy sweeps hurriedly through the underbrush, using her stick to push aside old leaves and pine needles. "This will do," she announces, lifting one end of a sturdy spruce branch.

I grab the other end and we drag it back to the Jeep.

Delphy studies the vehicle and the tree it's leaning against, and announces that we need to get "high purchase."

"What's that?" I ask.

"Best place to put the lever. Up high, just under where it meets the tree. Come around to this side and help me."

The branch is about six inches around and maybe ten feet long and too heavy for one person to handle. With both of us sweating and grunting like weight lifters, we manage to jam the end in place.

"Hold the weight on your shoulder, like this," she tells me.

Harder for me because I'm shorter, but I manage to do it. And then we're pushing against the branch with all our might. Our backs are to the Jeep, so I can't see what's happening, but our big lever must be working, because I can feel the weight shifting. Then, suddenly, we're falling forward, scrambling to avoid having the big branch fall on us, and there's a whomping sound of steel and springs hitting the ground, hard.

The Jeep has landed upright, in a cloud of dust and pine needles. I walk around it, surveying the damage. The windshield is smashed, the headlights shattered, but all four tires are holding air.

We hurriedly grab the canned goods and jugs of water, and load them into the back of the Jeep, along with Delphy's backpack. The smoke makes my eyes sting.

"You think it will start?" she asks.

"Only one way to find out." I carefully climb into the

102

driver's seat and test the steering wheel. Feels solid. I push in the clutch, and then press my other foot against the starter pedal.

The engine turns over but doesn't start, and the battery sounds weak. I get out from behind the wheel.

"That's it? You're giving up?"

"I think it needs fuel. Like maybe the gas leaked out of the carburetor when it was tipped on its side."

Delphy helps me get the hood open. I'm trying not to panic with all the sweat and smoke. "Sam! Hurry up!"

I'm no mechanic, but I remember Dad working on his pickup truck, an older model, and adjusting the carburetor. Him explaining how it squirts gas into a mist that's inhaled by the cylinders. Or something like that. All I really know is that an engine needs fuel. "Delphy, pump the gas pedal." I put my ear to the carburetor, and hear the sound of squirting gas.

"Okay," I say, lowering the hood. "Give it a few minutes to make sure it isn't flooded and I'll try it again."

"Sam? We may not have a few minutes. Ouch!"

The falling ash now contains live sparks. I look up, and sure enough, some of the highest spruce branches are starting to wink into flame.

I slip behind the wheel, and give it a go. The starter turns over once, twice—and then the engine roars to life, and the next thing, we're speeding down that old logging trail under a shower of ash and sparks, me and Delphy and the Jeep, which seems to be as alive as we are.

24.

The Last Branch

Two or three miles down the trail and we're out from under the falling sparks, mostly. I say mostly, because much to my surprise, Delphy pours water on my head and then explains that my hair was starting to catch fire.

"You looked like a human candle," she says, very pleased with herself.

"It's not funny."

"It's kind of funny. A teeny little bit," she says, chuckling. "You can smile now, Sam. We made it. We escaped!"

I start to say, "Yeah, for now," but then decide to keep my mouth shut. Maybe she has the right idea—be happy when you get the chance, and never mind what may be coming around the next bend in the trail. But I can't help worrying about that. Look what one moose did to us! We'd probably have found a real road by now, if not for that moose. Add to that the mistake of chasing a plane that couldn't possibly see us through the tree cover, even if it was searching for us, which it obviously wasn't.

So far we've been lucky, keeping ahead of the fire. But sooner or later our luck will run out. We'll make a wrong turn, or make a bad decision, or the dirt bikers will catch up. One way or another we'll find ourselves surrounded by flames, and that will be it.

Sorry, Mom. I tried, I really did.

I'm haunted by the fact that we don't know where we are, other than somewhere to the north and west of where we started. We don't even know exactly where the fire is, or where it's going next. You'd have to be in a helicopter to see the shape of the fire. Visibility at ground level isn't much better than a hundred yards in the deep forest, and in some of the most overgrown areas, much less.

I push in the clutch and shift to neutral. We slow to a stop. Delphy looks anxious. "What's up?" she wants to know.

"Let's try the radio again. Maybe Phat Freddy has some good news."

Delphy nods, removes the little radio from her backpack, pulls out the antenna, and starts cranking. She presses the on button.

Static.

"Where on the dial?" she asks.

"Ninety-eight point six."

She tries fine-tuning, aiming the antenna around, but all we get is static.

"Maybe we're out of range," I say, trying not to sound

disappointed. "Or maybe he got rescued, or the generator ran out of fuel, or broke down."

"Maybe," she says doubtfully.

"I always thought it was funny, the way he talks about broadcasting from the 'lowest official mountain,' but even from the lowest mountain, he can probably see the fire coming from a long way off. He'll have time to get out of there."

"I hope so. The last time we tuned in, he sounded scared."

Thinking about height and visibility gives me an idea. I put the Jeep in first gear and let out the clutch. We trundle along at about ten miles an hour. I ask Delphy to keep an eye out for a tall straight tree with climbable branches.

"Are you crazy?" is her first response, and then she goes, "Oh, I get it. Maybe you can see where the fire is."

"Maybe. And I might even be able to spot a road if I get high enough."

"You have to promise you won't fall."

"I won't fall. I'm a good tree climber," I say. Which is only partly a fib. It's true I once climbed almost to the top of a tree outside our house. But it was a one-way trip—I was too scared to come down. Dad had to rescue me with a rickety extension ladder. Said I was worse than a cat, and if I tried it again, don't forget to bring a parachute.

Later, overhearing what he said to Mom, I realized he was as freaked as me. Dad was fearless about most things, and even though he never let me know it, he was scared to death I might fall before he got to me.

Finding the right sort of tree turns out to be harder than I thought. Delphy spots some really tall pines—white pines are the official state tree—but most of them don't have branches low enough to grab. It's not like we have climbing gear, or even ropes. So it has to be a tree where I can climb branch to branch, and high enough to get a clear view over the top of the forest.

After fifteen minutes or so of searching, Delphy points into the woods. "Slow down. How about that one?"

"Branches are too high."

"Yeah, but see that tree growing next to it? Leaning on it, actually?"

I stop and turn off the engine. "Might work. Let's check it out."

The closer we get, the better it looks. The big tree rises straight up through the forest, and has lots of sturdy-looking branches starting at about thirty feet off the ground. And leaning up against it, like a boxer that lost a fight, is an old, twisted tree with branches that are barely over my head.

"You sure you want to do this?" Delphy peers up into the mass of branches. "It looks pretty sketchy."

"No problem. If I get stuck, just call the fire department."

"Ha ha. Seriously, though, it looks dangerous."

"I'll be fine." I grab hold of the lowest branch.

Delphy gives me a boost and I swing over on top of the branch and then scoot along on my stomach, arms wrapped around until I get to the main trunk. Then I stand up and start climbing branch to branch. Always holding on with both hands.

The old tree is so close to the big pine that switching over to the taller tree is easier than I thought. They say if you're scared of heights, you should never look down. Not a problem in this case, because the branches are so full that all I can see below me is boughs thick with pine needles. They look almost soft, like if I fell, the boughs would catch me. And maybe they would. Not that I want to find out. No, I'm being as careful as possible, my hands sticky with pinesap from holding on so tight.

Every so often, Delphy shouts from below to ask if I'm okay, and I shout back. Her voice sounds farther and farther away, and still I can't see through the surrounding trees. Pausing to look up, I decide a few more branches in height will put me in the clear, or as clear as it's going to get unless I go all the way to the top, which is impossible. Too skinny up there, too waving-in-the-wind. Just two more branches, that's all I need to see my way clear.

The last branch is the one that almost kills me.

25.

Home, Sweet Home

It happened so fast I can't hardly put it together in my head. I'd gone as high as I was going to go. Then I tried to stand up, and my sweaty hands lost their grip. Next thing I'm on my belly, gripping the branch for dear life and struggling to catch my breath because the wind has been knocked out of me.

Close call. Way too close.

I wrap my arms and legs around the branch and close my eyes and tell myself to be calm. A bad thing almost happened, but it didn't. Slowly the air comes back into my lungs, and my heart slows down to something like normal. Sweat drips from the end of my nose, splashing on the pine needles one branch below.

On the ground, at the base of the tree, Delphy shouts, "Sam! Are you okay? The whole tree shook! Sam! Sam!"

Takes a while to gather enough strength to reply. "I'm okay! Just slipped is all!"

Delphy isn't visible—too many branches in the way—but I can picture her expression as she shouts up, "You better not fall, Sam! If you fall, I'll kill you, understand? Promise me you won't fall!"

"I promise!"

"Come down! Please?"

Probably I'd be as worried if she was up the tree and I was on the ground. But there's no way I'm coming back down until I've seen whatever there is to see. So I gather my strength, and tell myself it will be okay as long as I'm super careful, and then very slowly I stand up, gripping the pine boughs to keep my balance.

Imagine your head is a periscope rising just above the treetops. One moment you're blind, and then you can see for miles.

And, oh, what a sight!

I can't wait to tell Delphy.

I won't bore you with the climb down, other than to say it was about twice as hard as going up. Yes, I did slip a time or three, but never quite lost my grip, so that's all that counts.

At the bottom, Delphy drops her stick and wraps both arms around me for a quick hug. "You made it. What if you got stuck? It's not like I can call for a rescue."

"I didn't get stuck. But I did see the fire."

"Close?"

"Not close at all. At least ten miles away, just barely visible along the horizon. Some of the smoke is blowing this direction, but the wind is settling down, so it's not spreading fast. Best thing, there's a lake or pond a few miles from here. I saw buildings, Delphy, a bunch of buildings! A big shingled main building and lots of little white cabins. I'm pretty sure it's a summer camp!"

"Are you serious?" Her eyes are as big as Christmas morning.

"Which means there has to be a real road nearby, right? To supply the camp? It's not like parents are going to hike through the woods to see their kids."

"This is so cool." The words catch in her throat. "You said it's not far away?"

"Maybe four or five miles as the crow flies. Too far to risk getting lost again in the woods. We'll have to follow the logging trail and hope it meets up with the real road. We might not make it before the sun goes down, but I'm a thousand percent sure this will be our last night without a roof over our heads."

"A thousand percent?"

"More like a million percent. We're almost there, Delphy, I promise."

"You think the camp will have hot showers? And real food and phones?" she asks, and then adds, "Are there people there? Did you see cars?"

Eager to get going, I head for the Jeep. As usual, Delphy matches me stride for stride, loping along with a big smile on her face and her dark eyes shining. I've never seen her so happy. It makes her look sort of beautiful, in a dirt-smudged, spent-the-night-leaning-against-a-tree, coated-with-smoke kind of way.

"No, I didn't see cars or people. They probably evacuated. But if it happened like at Camp Wabanaski, a lot of the food and water and maybe even fuel got left behind. The important thing, there has to be a road to get to the camp. A real road that leads to a bigger road that gets us to the highway. Phone chargers and hamburgers! Civilization!"

"Home, sweet home." Delphy sits up straight, shoulders back, ready for anything. "I never knew what that meant, not really, but now I do."

We drive down the logging trail. Our luck has turned and I'm feeling good about it.

What an idiot.

26.

The Tree House

As we lurch slowly along, avoiding potholes and tire-busting rocks in the fading light, Delphy has this fierce look on her face, like she wants to hold back the sunset. Like if she concentrates really hard, the sun will stay up long enough for us to find the summer camp.

I feel rotten about it, but there's no way we're going to get there before the sun goes down. And we can't drive a rutted trail like this in the dark, especially with smashed headlights. No way.

When I suggest that we may have to pull over and wait until morning, she takes offense.

"Are you serious? Sleep in this smelly little Jeep? In case you haven't noticed, I'm a big girl. Tall and big, remember? I barely fit in this seat as it is, and there's no room to stretch out my legs."

"Don't be mad." I slow the Jeep to a crawl.

"Who says I'm mad? Really, that's what you think?" She takes a deep breath. "Okay, maybe a little bit mad. It's just my ankle hurts wicked bad, and I really, really, really need a hot shower."

"Soon," I promise. "Soon."

"One thing's for sure, I'm not sleeping sitting up. Not again. Not when there's a tree house available."

She must be joking, right? But then she points, and for the first time I notice an enclosed platform built between two trees not far from the trail. Not a tree house. A deer stand.

The stand is nothing fancy, just a plywood platform, maybe ten feet off the ground, with four canvas walls daubed for camouflage, which makes it hard to see. Hunters use it to spot deer. Part of an old aluminum extension ladder is tied to the platform with a piece of rope. Delphy goes first, and I hand up her backpack and then scramble into the thing. The floor is creaky and covered with old pine needles, but she's right: It's better than sleeping up against a tree, or in the Jeep.

"We should pull the ladder up."

"Why bother?" she says.

"Bears."

She makes a face. "You said not to worry about bears."

"I lied."

We pull up the ladder and tie it sideways to the edge of the platform.

"Bears or no bears, this is sort of fun." She stretches out her long legs. "Like playing fort in the backyard."

"You played fort?"

"Sure. Me and the twins. They'd pretend they'd captured the Big Friendly Giant. The best part was when I escaped and knocked down the fort. Stomped it like Godzilla, which is way more fun than being the BFG. Then we'd put it back together and do the same thing all over again. Kids!"

"Yeah, kids."

I'm relieved her mood has improved. Plus, we have cans of tuna and a full jug of water. May not sound like much, but when you're famished and thirsty, it goes down like Thanksgiving dinner with all the trimmings. Or that's what we tell ourselves.

"Tur-keee. Mash potatoes and gray-vee . . . mmm, mmm, mmm." I'm doing my best Homer Simpson impersonation.

Delphy laughs. It's full dark, with no stars visible through the dense canopy of trees, so I can't see her face. But I know her mood has changed by the tone of her voice. "You know what's weird? They probably think we're dead. My parents and your mother. My little sisters. All our friends. They're planning our funerals. Feeling sorry for all the mean things they said to us." She pauses. "I don't mean you. I'm talking about my so-called friends."

"Everybody says rotten things sometimes. It doesn't mean they're not friends. But you're right, my mom probably thinks the worst."

She chuckles. "That's so you, Sam. You're the one in bad trouble, but you're more worried about your mother."

I almost tell her, but then decide to hold it back. I don't want her feeling sorry for me, the pathetic kid with the dead father and the drug-addict mom. Because it's not like that. I can't explain why, exactly, but it's not.

No idea how long it took to fall asleep, but when the first explosion hits, lighting up the forest, I'm curled up in some scratchy old pine needles, and Delphy is screaming my name.

Day Five

27.

Snake Lightning

The heat storm is so close there's no delay between the flashes and the booming thunder. It's like we're inside the lightning. The flashes turn the canvas walls transparent, cracking brighter and brighter, and I expect that any second a sizzling bolt will hit us directly and the deer stand will explode.

I want to tell Delphy not to be afraid, but I'm too scared to talk. She grabs my hand and squeezes so hard I think she's going to break it. The trees are shivering all around us, as if they're as terrified as we are.

There's no wind or rain, just hot, humid air alive with electricity. Mighty bolts crack open the early morning sky, thumping the earth like hammer blows.

A bolt strikes close by, with a cracking boom that could be the world splitting open. So loud my ears hurt. A tree groans and splinters and falls, crashing into more trees on the way down. We see the hot glowing sparks of it burning from the inside.

We've been running away from the fire, putting miles between it and us, but now it has found us.

The deer stand begins to shake and rumble as more falling trees brush by.

Delphy shouts, "We better get out of here!"

I'm about to slide the aluminum ladder to the ground when the hair lifts on my head. My scalp tingles in a strange way, and I drop the ladder just as everything goes sun-blaze white. A bolt snakes down the tree right next to us and explodes into the ground with the sound of a million M-80s going off at exactly the same moment. The tree roots begin to glow and smolder like fiery finger bones.

If I'd been holding the ladder, the lightning might have gone through me on the way to the ground.

Delphy is standing up, shaking her fist at the sky and screaming, "STOP! STOP!"

I try to pull her down, but she's stronger than me, and more angry at the thing that scares her.

"On the floor!" I beg her. "That's the safest place! Keep a low profile."

I'm not sure if it really is the safest place, but raising a fist to a lightning bolt has got to be more dangerous than lying flat on your face with your hands protecting your ears.

Let it stop, please make it go away.

And after what feels like an eternity, it does go away, rumbling off into the distance. Heading for the fire line, as if it wants to join in the fun of burning down the forest.

Delphy, face to the floor, says, "Is it safe? Are we alive?"

"Yeah, we made it. But there's one little problem. The ladder fell to the ground. I, um, dropped it."

She slowly shakes her head, as if to say, *What next?*

I lean out the opening, into a whiff of smoke from the smoldering roots. Ground is maybe ten feet below. If I were to jump, there's a chance I'd sprain or break both ankles. Instead, I get down on my belly and carefully lower myself from the platform until I'm hanging on by my clenched hands. So, according to my semi-panicked calculations, the ground is five feet or less beneath my dangling feet.

I let go, landing feetfirst in the layer of pine needles, and then tumble over backward. It hurts, but nothing is broken. I limp over to the ladder and lean it up against the opening. Delphy peers down at me. "You're crazy, you know that?"

"No choice!" I say, feeling good about my decision.

I hold the ladder as she descends. I can tell her ankle hurts as she puts weight on it, but she doesn't complain. She fusses around until she finds her walking stick and looks back up at the tree stand.

"Sam? We need to get out of here. Like right now!"

I look up. The canvas walls of the deer stand have caught fire. Our refuge is going up in flames! The fire is already spreading. Not fast, not yet. But it will grow and feed on itself, tree by root by tree, and within an hour or two it will become a new, full-scale wildfire.

We're hurrying to the Jeep when Delphy says, "What's that smell?"

"Probably me."

"Not a boy smell," she says, puzzled. "More like a zoo." Her dark, shining eyes get big and round. "Uh-oh."

"Uh-oh, what?" I say, but then I see it, rising up in the back seat.

A black bear, looking at me like he's starving and I'm breakfast.

28.

The Only Way to Stay Alive

On my hikes with Dad, he explained what to do if I ever came across a bear. "The black bear is a complicated creature," he would say. "In this part of the world, a full-grown bear has no real predators, other than us. So if you meet one on the trail, don't run. It might chase you, and you can't outrun a bear. Hold your ground and the bear will likely leave."

Great advice if you happen to sight a bear in the woods or on a trail, or even in your own backyard. But not in the vehicle you desperately need to escape from a smoldering fire that's going to burst into full-blown flames any second.

Trying not to make any sudden or threatening moves, I whisper, "Delphy? Back up, slowly."

We stop about twenty yards away. The air is thickening with smoke.

"It doesn't want to leave." Delphy shifts her stick. "It's scared, I think."

The bear is upright in the back seat now, nodding its head back and forth, back and forth. Not full-grown but not a cub, either. Probably scared, like Delphy says. Scared of the storm, scared of the fire. No cave or den for shelter, so it picked the Jeep.

And scared is when a bear is most dangerous. Like Dad said, usually a bear will run away rather than confront a human. But if it doesn't, things can get ugly quick.

"I don't know what to do! Should we leave the Jeep and run?"

Then Delphy does something I never would have expected, or I'd have tried to stop her. She marches up to the Jeep and uses her stick to press on the horn. She stands her ground, making the horn blare. And the bear bolts out of the back seat and scampers off into the woods, away from the fire.

"Nice meeting you, bear!" she calls out, then climbs into the passenger seat, waiting for me.

I get in. "That was really dangerous."

She smiles, as pleased with herself as I was for jumping from the deer stand. "Everything we do is dangerous. It's the only way to stay alive."

We drive down the logging trail, away from the smoke. The forest gets a little thinner and more of the sky is visible over our heads. The sunshine makes it even hotter, which hardly seems possible. The trail becomes straighter, and we seem to be on a ridge, with the ground falling away on either side. Not exactly climbing a mountain, but on higher ground for sure.

Everything is going really good until the engine sputters and dies.

Out of gas. It finally happened.

Delphy doesn't say anything. We just sit there for a while, baking in the airless heat. We should be really upset, but for some reason we're not. Maybe the storm and the fire and the bear was all the upset we could handle.

"Shall we take a little walk?" Delphy suggests.

She slings her backpack over her shoulder, gets a good grip on her walking stick, and off we go, following the logging trail. No way am I going back in the woods, even if it isn't quite so dense.

The trail curves gently to the right. For a while, it keeps level and then starts to head down.

We both see it at the same time, glittering through the trees.

A long blue lake.

29.

The Bell

We work our way down the wooded slope to the curving shoreline. Delphy drops her walking stick and backpack. She keeps going, right into the water, and doesn't stop until she's waist-high. "You have to do it, Sam," she says, waving me to join her. "It's amazing."

I cast a wary eye for water snakes, but they like muddy bottoms and weeds and this is clear and sandy. Too inviting to resist. I don't go in as deep as Delphy, not being as tall, but after days on the run, in the constant heat, the cool clean water is like heaven. I bend my knees and sink down, holding my breath as my head goes under. Amazing is right.

I come up spouting.

Delphy smooths the wet hair out of her eyes. "Where's the camp?" she asks. "Which way?"

I close my eyes and picture what I saw from the top of the tree. "That way." I point. "Somewhere along this shore."

"Is it far?"

"I don't know. A few miles? Maybe less."

We slog out of the water. I start to shake myself dry and

Delphy goes, "Hey, wait! My beach towel!" She pulls it out of the backpack and tosses it to me. "You first."

I rub down fast and hand it back.

"Not what I had in mind when I thought I was going for a midnight swim." Delphy, drying her hair, sounds almost cheerful. "Jason Dean, you don't know what you missed."

Should I tell her Jason Dean doesn't exist? No, I don't want to hurt her feelings. She's smart. She'll figure it out.

I take off my shoes, dry them on the grass, and put them back on. Soggy, but tolerable. The only bad thing is the mosquitoes, but Delphy is in such a good mood, getting bit doesn't seem to bother her. "Take a sip, everybody!" She holds her arms out to the bugs. "Come one, come all!"

"You're crazy."

"Crazy happy. There's a difference."

We prepare ourselves for a long hike, but the camp is much closer than I thought. Around the next bend, we come upon a curving notch of shoreline with a white sandy beach and volleyball courts. Back from the lake is a big, white-shingled building with two huge stone chimneys, one on each end. Along the edge of the lake are a dozen or so smaller buildings, similar to the cabins at Camp Wabanaski.

"Hello!" I shout. "Anybody home?"

Silence. As to be expected, the place was evacuated. We work our way around the main building, still shouting in case somebody stayed behind, and locate the entrance, which has a big banner strung along the porch roof:

Delphy shakes her head, laughing. "Just my luck, a survival camp. They probably eat nuts and berries."

"There's a dining hall inside." I'm peering through the windows. "Check it out. Maybe you can find a phone. I'll look for a road."

"You want me to do the breaking and entering, is that it?" She sounds amused.

I try the latch. "No breaking required." I swing open the unlocked door for her and turn to go. As I head out to look for a road, she cautions me. "Be careful."

"Always. I won't be long."

A neatly landscaped gravel drive runs off into the woods, heading uphill. Could be several miles to a paved road, but I want to get some idea of what we're up against. It's really great we found the camp, which means shelter and water and probably food, even if it *is* nuts and berries, but there's a tinge of smoke in the air, and we can't be that many miles from the spreading lightning fire, or for that matter from the main fire line behind it. So the camp is temporary shelter, at best.

I start out jogging along the gravel road, hoping I can find some gasoline in the camp and a way to get the Jeep down from the logging trail. The lawns are mowed, so they must have power mowers, right? Unless survival camp means push mowers. Which is possible. No, don't think that way. Be positive. One thing at a time. See where the gravel road goes, then worry about the Jeep.

I jog uphill for a mile or so in the crushing heat, sweat pouring into my eyes, until I get this pain in my side that feels like a knife shoved into my ribs. I rest for a bit, bent over and panting, and the pain eases. Okay, so I'm not exactly a track star. And I'm thinking maybe I don't want to get too far along the gravel roadway, not just yet. What if I get cut off by the fire? Delphy on one side of the flames, me on the other?

It's when I turn to go back that I notice the sign. Must have missed it with my eyes full of sweat. A little arrow-shaped sign nailed to a tree. Hand-painted but easy to read.

SR 12B—7.2 MILES

State Road 12B. No clue as to where it might lead, but chances are it will be a real paved road. It has to go somewhere that's populated, or the state wouldn't bother building a road, right? Somewhere with people, that's all that matters.

I'm walking briskly when a bell begins to ring. Like the shimmering bong of a church bell, but that can't be it. Maybe it's an emergency signal. Maybe Delphy's in trouble.

I start running.

30.

In Case of Fire

Turns out to be a dinner bell, not an emergency signal. Delphy noticed the rope hanging in a corner of the dining room and rang the bell to let me know there's enough food in the pantry to last a year, at least.

"Ten kinds of cereal, five kinds of cookies. Canned goods galore, in big restaurant cans. Vegetables, meats, soups, sauces. At least five dozen eggs. Flour and cornmeal and baking powder and tons of ingredients to make stuff. No electricity— I don't think this place has any—but the stoves and refrigerators run on propane, and they have a huge tank of propane out back, so we're good there. Fridges packed with gallon jugs of milk, at least ten pounds of butter, trays of Jell-O, blocks of processed cheese."

"All that, but no phone?"

She shakes her head and sighs. "We're out in the middle of nowhere. No landlines, and like I said, no electricity. The lamps use oil, I think. They're not kidding about being into survival."

We're in the dining hall, which looks like it could seat fifty or so, easy, with a soaring cathedral roof made out of hand-carved wood beams, and very cool stone fireplaces on opposite walls, and a view of the long, narrow lake that shoots out from the beach like a blue arrow aimed at the horizon. It's a grand room, way better than the dining area at Camp Wabanaski, and a bit cooler than outside. My guess, the camp caters to out-of-state families with kids who need a little toughening up, or who want an adventure. Cold-water showers—Delphy already checked—and lots of activities like hiking, climbing, and learning to live off the land. So Delphy had it right when she said nuts and berries.

Not that anybody is going hungry, not when they're eating in this dining hall, that's for sure. But the no-electricity setup makes me wonder, because summer camps have to be able to alert the authorities or call for an ambulance—at this location, probably by air—if one of the kids gets seriously ill or injured. Right? When I mention this to Delphy she goes, "Cell phones?"

"Maybe," I say. "But way out here? Where are the cell towers?"

"Smoke signals?"

That makes me grin. "Ha ha. I'm thinking maybe some kind of two-way emergency radio. The kind you can talk on. Maybe a police radio kind of deal. They knew enough to evacuate, right?"

"That makes sense."

134

"Okay, if it was you in charge, where would you keep the emergency radio?"

She thinks about it. "The office? I saw a room that could be the office, out by the main entrance."

She leads me to it and I agree, this has to be the camp office. A wooden desk and a big swivel chair, several filing cabinets, and knotty pine walls plastered with photographs of kids on survival trips. White-water rafting, canoe portaging, rock climbing with helmets and harnesses and complicated-looking ropes. The kids look happy to be working so hard—most are pumping fists in the air. There's a good-sized map pinned to a corkboard. Marvel Lake Survival Skills Camp is marked on the map with a red star, and it shows the access road connecting to the state road, just like the sign said. It also shows we're about as far to the north and west as you can get and still be in Maine.

I point to the star and say, "That's why the only station we can pick up is WRPZ. We're pretty much in the middle of nowhere, surrounded by mountains."

"Mountains that are burning," Delphy reminds me.

Tinder-dry forests. Wildfires. I'd rather not think about it, but there's no getting away from the fact that a clock is ticking. We have to find a way to get rescued, or rescue ourselves, before the fire finds us.

We search everywhere. The shelves are packed with books about birds and wildlife, but there's no sign of a two-way police radio.

Delphy opens all the desk drawers. No electronics. But she does find an instruction manual for a satellite phone.

I slump into the swivel chair, exasperated. "That's how they make contact. A satellite phone. Probably took it with them when they evacuated."

"Definitely." Delphy looks as disappointed as I feel.

"It's okay." I'm trying to sound upbeat. "Back to plan A. We're only seven miles from a paved road. If I can find some gas, and a way to get the Jeep over to the gravel road, we can be back to civilization in an hour."

She brightens. "Seriously? If you can't find any gas, I can walk seven miles if I have to. I don't care how much it hurts, if it will get us home."

"Let's find some gas. Hiking seven miles on a sprained ankle is a bad idea. What if the fire catches up and crosses the gravel road before we get there? No way to outrace a fire on foot. If it comes to that, we might be better off staying right where we are: In case of fire, jump in the lake and hope the smoke doesn't kill us."

"Where do we start?" she asks.

"With fuel of our own. Did you say there are five kinds of cookies?"

After eating—cookies plus a couple of premade salami sandwiches we find in the big refrigerators (Delphy even locates some ballpark mustard. I swear it's the best sandwich I've ever had in my life)—it's down to business.

The search for gasoline. Which we absolutely need to make an escape.

When I ask her to take it easy and rest her ankle, Delphy gives me an are-you-crazy? look, props herself on her stick, and swings down the steps onto the lawn.

"You take that side, I'll take this one," she says. "We're looking for sheds and storage areas, right?"

"And lawn mowers and chain saws and weed whackers. Like that. They all need gas."

I remember seeing some storage units next to one of the cabins. Before heading to check it out, I study the horizon to the east, beyond the far end of the lake. I don't want Delphy to worry about it too much, but for the last hour or so, gray clouds have been edging up over the horizon.

Are they storm clouds or distant smoke? Rain or fire? Can't be sure, one way or the other. Whatever they are, they seem to be slowly creeping closer.

31.

Another Greek Thing

Delphy is so into it, I'm almost sorry it's me who finds the gasoline. Twenty gallons, neatly lined up in red five-gallon plastic containers, with spouts and funnels. Fuel for a big, professional mowing machine housed in the shed.

She hobbles in, sees me beaming, and goes, "Is that enough?"

"Enough for two hundred miles. We can drive all the way home on this amount."

"I thought you said it was only seven miles?"

"Seven to a paved road. Not sure how far that is from getting rescued. But this will get us there, I promise."

She folds her arms across her chest. "Today?"

"Yes, today, if I can find a way to connect the Jeep up to the gravel road."

She shakes her head, amused. "If there's one thing I've learned in the last few days, it's that you always find a way. You go, I'll pack up whatever supplies I can scrounge, and when you get back here—zoom, we're gone!"

What she said about me always finding a way makes me feel really good, and gives me the energy to start lugging a five-gallon can up the slope to the logging trail. Panting and sweating and keeping an eye out on the way for a path big enough for the Jeep. The slope is okay for walking, but there are parts too steep for any vehicle, even a sturdy Jeep. I'm being super careful, because the Jeep is our only hope of escape. The fire may not be moving very fast today, with the wind so calm, but it's getting closer. I can feel it. I can smell it. I know it in my bones.

I finally haul the heavy container up to the logging trail, and there's the Jeep, waiting patiently. Okay, I'm aware it's only a hunk of steel, and it doesn't have a mind of its own, and it can't be "waiting patiently." But I feel like we're connected somehow, me and that machine. From the very first, when we sped away from the flames at the logging camp and I barely knew how to steer, it's like the machine was taking care of me. Like it had been waiting for a chance to save my life.

Delphy isn't there to hear me being weird, so as I pour gas into the tank, me and the Jeep have a one-sided conversation. "Once we get rescued, you'll have to go back to your real owner. I know that. But maybe he'll let me visit. And when I'm old enough to get a driver's license, maybe I'll have saved up enough to buy you. Would that be okay?"

In my head, the Jeep says yes. Which is just me saying yes, but still it makes me feel better. Without this brave

140

little machine, made for a soldier in a long-ago war, me and Delphy would be dead for sure. So forgive me if I get all mushy about it.

On second thought, I don't care what anybody thinks. The Jeep is my friend, get used to it.

With five gallons in the tank, the Jeep is good to go. It starts right up, and I slowly steer along the rutted logging trail, searching for a place where we can cross down the slope to Camp Survival.

Sounds like it should be easy, but it isn't. Everywhere I look, it seems to be either too steep and rocky, or too thick with trees. I can't risk getting stuck halfway down. Can't risk making a mistake. This is our chance, this hunk of steel and tires, and every instinct tells me I have to treat it like it's made of glass. It may be tough and reliable, but things can go wrong in an instant.

The old logging trail slowly curves down toward the lake. There are fewer trees blocking the way to the camp. The main building is clearly visible through the thinning trees, and beside it the gravel road, maybe a quarter mile away.

So close.

I get out and explore on foot. No problem navigating around the trees or avoiding the boulders strewn through this part of the forest. The problem is right at the end, where the woodlands meet the camp lawn. There's about a four-foot drop over a steep, rocky ledge. No way to get past that without ripping out the bottom of the Jeep and breaking an axle.

Delphy sees me exploring along the edge and lopes over, swinging on her stick. She's excited to see the Jeep so near, just a little ways uphill through the trees.

"I've put together a bunch of supplies. Food and water and stuff. And if you must know, more TP. Just in case the road is long."

"Great," I say, without much enthusiasm.

"What's wrong?"

"This is as close as the logging trail gets to the camp," I explain, discouraged. "Beyond this, it starts to curve away, up into the hills. So the Jeep has to cross over in this area. Somehow. Except I don't know how."

Delphy swings along on her walking stick, examining the rocky ledge. "I see what you mean. The only way down is to build a ramp."

"Great," I say. "I'll fire up the bulldozer. Oh, wait, we don't have a bulldozer."

Delphy sees the look on my face and laughs. "We don't need a bulldozer, silly. We just need an inclined plane."

"Is that another ancient Greek thing?"

"As a matter of fact, yes. By way of Egypt."

32.

What Scares You Most

O ver the next few hours, we pry a couple of long, sturdy planks from the walkway to the dock, drag them across the lawn, and prop them on the ledge. Then we roll a bunch of rocks into place under the middle of the planks, for support. On paper, an inclined plane is just a few pencil lines. In the real world, building one takes time and tons of sweat, especially when it's so miserably hot.

Delphy explains how some of the pyramids were constructed. "They hauled giant limestone blocks up very long, inclined planes. Took them twenty years and thousands of laborers."

"And this comes from your grandfather?"

She laughs. "I saw it on the History Channel."

I collapse on the lawn, exhausted. The sun is about to dip below the tree line, and we both understand that inching the Jeep down the slope and onto the planks will have to wait until morning. It's not a thing that can be done in the dark, or when we're too tired to think straight.

"First thing, right?"

"First thing. Before I quit, I'm going to bring up the rest of the gas and fill the tank. Just in case."

"In case of what?" Delphy asks, uneasy.

"Just in case."

When that last task is done, and the Jeep has a full tank with an extra can to spare, I unplug the distributor wire like before. Because you never know, and no spark means no steal.

I'm so tired it feels like there are ten-pound weights around my ankles as I trudge back to the dining hall. We use wooden matches to light a couple of the oil lanterns and munch on some more cookies and drain glasses of cold milk. "Not exactly a balanced meal." Delphy smiles, her eyes bright. "At Calusa, we had to earn desserts by exercising."

"You just exercised enough to build a small pyramid."

"I guess I did, didn't I? Who knew? I totally hate gym, but when I really have to, I can move a two-ton Jeep."

"Mostly with your brain. You figure things out."

She mock punches me in the arm. "We're a pretty good team."

"Yup."

"A toast to us, little brother." She clinks her glass of milk to mine. "To getting home tomorrow."

"Tomorrow."

Delphy fishes through her backpack and takes out the little hand-crank radio. "Maybe there's news about the fire. News about the world."

She works the crank, charging the battery, and when she pushes the on button, what do you know, WRPZ comes through loud and clear! Almost sounds like the DJ is in the dining hall with us, sharing milk and cookies while he tells us about his day.

"... no idea who might be in range of my voice because, like I said, the broadcast radius of this little station is much reduced. The main power lines are down and we're running on the backup generator. I say 'we,' but it's only me, your host, Phat Freddy Bell. And to be honest, I wouldn't be trapped here if I didn't drain all the gas from my car to power the generator. Which is just about to run out of fuel anyhow. Bonehead move. I'm surrounded, folks. Fire on every side. And nobody trying to stop it. Not that I'm complaining. Our brave firefighters are concentrating on the populated areas to the south, where the flames have consumed part of Belfast, Belmont, and Waldo, resulting in fatalities for civilians and firefighters alike. So it looks like I'm stuck here at six hundred and one feet above groove level until the fire burns out. And if I don't make it, I just want everybody to know—my listeners, my friends, my late wife in heaven, everybody—that it's been a blast sharing my favorite tunes, connecting with

145

listeners. I loved every minute of it. I'm the luckiest man in the world, and who knows, maybe my luck will hold.

"This is Phat Freddy Bell, high atop the lowest official mountain in the great state of Maine, signing off."

We're left with only our own silence to fill the room.

Delphy wipes her eyes with the side of her hand. "Poor guy, he sounded scared."

"Somebody is bound to hear him and go to the rescue."

"I hope so."

Something the DJ said really shakes me. All this time I'd been worried about me and Delphy getting burned up, but it turns out the fire is eating towns and cities, not just forest. Belfast, Belmont, Waldo. Phat Freddy didn't mention Portland, where my mother is in rehab, but I can't help worrying that maybe she's in danger, too.

For the last few days, it's seemed like the fire was concentrating on us, but it sounds like there's a lot more going on that we don't know about.

Like the whole state is up in flames.

Delphy has this expression on her face, like she knows what I'm thinking, and shares my concern. "Can I ask you a question, Sam?"

"Sure." I dread what she might ask.

"What scares you most?"

33.

Stuff to Worry About

"That's not fair, so I'll go first." Delphy takes a deep breath, and then she blurts out, "I'm scared I'll never stop growing."

"Seriously?"

"Silly, I know. Most girls stop growing by the time they're fifteen. And I'm almost fifteen, and I haven't grown recently. So I'm worried about nothing. Probably."

"What's the big deal if you get a little taller?"

She sighs. "A little would be okay, I guess. But I had this nightmare that I was so tall my head was bumping the ceiling. I was like eight feet tall. Everybody was staring at me and whispering behind my back. It was awful. When I woke up, I was afraid to get out of bed, in case my head bumped."

I'm not sure how to answer, so I go, "Wow," and then shut up.

For some reason, that makes her laugh. "Don't worry, Sam. You don't have to tell me your greatest fear just because I told you mine. That was unfair, putting you on the spot."

Her eyes are so sad and kind that something breaks inside me, and I find myself gushing the truth. "I'm afraid my mother is going to die of an overdose."

Delphy's jaw drops. "Oh, Sam. No. That's terrible!"

The only other person who has any idea of what I really worry about is Mrs. Labrie, from Child Services, so it's kind of a relief, saying it out loud.

"When I wake up in the morning, I'm scared of finding her dead in her bed, or in the bathroom. When I'm in school, I'm afraid of what I'll find when I get home."

"That really sucks. I'm so sorry."

"That's why I was at Camp Wabanaski. So Mom could get treatment. She wants to quit, she really does. But it's really, really hard. Like the hardest thing in the world. That's what Mom said. She's sick and in pain and her whole body aches for the medicine. She says the medicine is like a giant magnet and she's an iron filing. And she says most addicts don't make it the first time they quit."

Delphy reaches across the table and covers my hands with hers. "I'll bet you anything she does. You're a strong, smart kid, and at least half of that comes from your mother, right?"

"Right."

"You know what's really dumb?" Delphy says brightly. "Here we are in the middle of nowhere, surrounded by a deadly forest fire, and what do we worry about? Stuff we can't control. When really the only thing we should worry about right now is how to stay alive! How do we get home?"

Big questions. I wish I knew the answers.

I wait on the front porch while Delphy goes to take a cold shower. Figure I'll take one tomorrow morning before we get to work on moving the Jeep. Besides, it gives me a chance to be alone for a few minutes when I can maybe organize my thoughts, get my head straight. Also keep an eye on the far end of the lake, making sure nothing flares or sparks.

So far so good. The usual scent of distant smoke, but nothing lighting up the darkness. Not yet.

Delphy returns from her shower sounding disappointed. "I thought cool water would cool me down, right? But as soon as I dried off, I was sweating again. Can't believe I'm saying this, but I'm looking forward to winter."

"Totally. Give me ice and snow."

The neat thing about being the only two people in a camp made for at least fifty, plus staff, is that we each get a cabin to ourselves. Real beds, with sheets and mattresses and pillows.

We choose cabins closest to the lake. Great view. Not that we can see very much of it on a moonless, starless night. All we can really make out, carrying our oil lanterns, is the path that goes from the main building to the cabins.

Delphy's cabin is called "Fortitude." Mine is called "Endurance."

"Real cozy," Delphy says sarcastically as she holds her lantern up to the sign.

"Must be like a message to inspire the campers. 'This is what you need to survive.'"

"What I need is a good night's sleep." She yawns. "First thing tomorrow, we get the Jeep down the incline, load it up, and head back to civilization. Part of me is almost sorry, you know?"

"Not me. I'm ready."

"You know what I've been thinking about, when I'm not being scared to death? A cheeseburger with a vanilla shake. First stop. Okay?"

"Deal."

We say our good nights and go to our cabins. Inside, I have my choice of bunks, and pick the one that's the most neatly made. I lie facedown, expecting to fall asleep in an instant, but my head is swirling with a million thoughts. It's like I'm too tired to sleep, which doesn't make any sense.

I turn the oil lantern off and sit on the edge of the bunk in the dark. Thinking about my mom and my dad, and now Delphy, who seems like part of the family somehow. How everything keeps whirling out of reach and I keep grabbing at it, but I can't hold on. It's so hard not to worry about things you can't possibly control.

Mrs. Labrie says that's what life is all about, learning how to deal with stuff you can't control. She's probably right, but that doesn't make it any easier. Not when I feel like I ran a marathon, swam the English Channel, and built the pyramids all in one day, and still I can't sleep.

I get up in the dark and walk to the window and there it is. A faint glow on the night horizon, maybe ten miles away.

Fire, on the other side of the mountains.

I finally fall asleep praying that the wind will change and blow the fire out like a candle on a birthday cake.

Day Six

34.

Burn, Baby, Burn

In my dream, Mom and I are at the beach, sitting in folding chairs with our feet in the water. We're watching Dad paddle around on a red rubber raft, acting goofy for our amusement. When Dad comes back to shore, the three of us will walk down to the hot dog stand and order extra-large onion rings with our dogs. It's the best day ever, and can't be spoiled, not even by the sound of crazy chain saws. I mean, who brings chain saws to the beach?

I wake up with someone's hand over my mouth. It's Delphy, hushing me. "Quiet," she whispers. "They're right outside."

The dream was just a dream, but the crazy chain-saw noise is real. Not chain saws, but dirt bikes roaring through the camp, and somebody shouting, "IF YOU'RE FROM AWAY, STAY AWAY! FROM AWAY, STAY AWAY!"

I sit up on the bunk, heart pounding. We crawl to a window and peep out at the main building. In the soft light of dawn, we can make out a biker doing a wheelie the full length of the porch, screaming his head off. No longer words, just a scream of rage.

On the front lawn, the other biker cheers him on, chanting, "FROM AWAY, STAY AWAY! FROM AWAY, STAY AWAY!"

Beside me, Delphy whispers, "It's them, isn't it? From Piney Pond? What's that supposed to mean, 'from away, stay away'?"

"Not sure, but I think it means they hate out-of-staters. People from away. People with money who come here and buy up the best land and build expensive places like this."

"And they think it's okay to burn them out, because they weren't born here?"

I shake my head. "I don't think they care about 'okay.' I mean, look at them."

These dudes were scary when they were on the other side of Piney Pond, torching a summer house, but up close they are terrifying. There's a madness about them, a violent fury at the people they're attacking. No helmets, and blond hair, both of them, shaved close on the sides and long on top. The light is still pretty dim, so I can't make out their faces, except for the beards, but from the way they act and move alike, I'm pretty sure they're brothers.

"Do they know we're here?" I whisper.

"Don't think so. I snuck around the back to get to this cabin. They didn't see me."

There's a crash of breaking glass, and suddenly they

invade the main building, on their bikes. We can't see what they're doing inside, exactly, but we can hear them zooming round and round, revving their engines. Every so often the bikes will pause, going to idle, and we hear the noise of something breaking, and their chant: "FROM AWAY, STAY AWAY! FROM AWAY, STAY AWAY!"

"This is probably crazy," Delphy says, "but what if we waded out into the lake? It's still kind of dark, chances are they won't notice us out there. And then even if the fire comes this way, we'd be safe."

"It's not crazy and it might work. But what if they stay until after sunrise, and spot us? And what about the smoke? Narrow lake like this, with hills on either side, the fire will spread from side to side. We'll be stuck, and we might not be able to breathe. Even if we can, how long will we last in deep water?"

"I hadn't thought about that," Delphy whispers. "What's your idea?"

"We should get out of here, hide in the woods until they leave."

"What if they see us?"

"We run. They won't be able to follow in the woods. If we make it to the Jeep, we can get away."

"I'm worried they'll spot me. Big and tall with a crutch, how can they miss that?"

Before I can think of an answer, something changes inside the main building. The biker brothers have turned on the lights. Which is impossible, with no electricity. And then

157

I realize they've discovered the lanterns and are scattering oil and lighting the place on fire, like they did to the house on Piney Pond. In less than a minute, the interior is so bright it hurts to look. The flames spread quickly, racing up the great beams of the cathedral ceiling and dripping down the beautiful wooden walls.

The brothers remain inside, admiring their work. Racing their dirt bikes around the dining hall, shouting, "From away, stay away! Burn, baby, burn!"

Any second, they'll have to exit the hall, or be trapped by the fire they started.

"Now's our chance," I whisper. "Their eyes are on the flames, they won't see us."

We creep out the back door, keeping the cabin between us and the main building. I look around the corner—they're still inside with the spreading flames, dangerous as it is—and we dash to the next cabin, and then to the next. Keeping to the shadows as we work our way around to the side of the camp where we'd propped up the planks and made an inclined plane.

Part of me wants to carry out our original plan. Get the Jeep across the inclined planks and over to the gravel road, and go from there. But the biker bros will see us for sure, and be on us in an instant. They probably came in on the gravel road and know this country way better than we do. So the only sensible thing to do is escape without being seen. Get to the Jeep, put some logging trail miles between us and the bikers.

I'm about to dash to the next cabin, when Delphy hisses, "Sam! Look!"

She's pointing at the lake. I've been so focused on the main house I haven't bothered to check out the lake. Small, tight waves are crashing along the shore, driven by the wind, which seems to be increasing with each beat of my heart. But Delphy's concern isn't the wind, at least not directly.

What's attracted her attention is the fire. Not the fire set by the bikers, but the main fire, the big fire, the one that's been chasing us for days. Last night, it was a faint glow on the horizon, miles away. This morning, the fire has speeded up. Now it's coming around both sides of the lake, trees burning from the top down. It can't be more than half a mile away, and moving fast.

All the more reason to get to the Jeep. If the biker bros torch the rest of the camp, we'll be surrounded by a circle of flame, with no way out. Do they know that? Do they even care?

At that moment, both bikes fly out of the building, onto the lawn. Behind them, windows explode with the heat, detonating like glass grenades. Black smoke billows out. They turn to admire their handiwork. Inside, beams begin to fall, and with each crash the building shudders and groans.

Now is our chance. We have to cover about a hundred yards of open lawn. If they glance back at the cabins, they'll see us for sure. Dangerous, but we can't stay where we are. Any place we could hide will soon be engulfed in flames.

Delphy straightens up, tucks her stick under her arm, and gives me a nod. "Whatever happens, don't look back," she says, and takes off at a lope, a brave girl, strong and tall.

35.

The Rabbit and the Wolf

We almost made it. The main building was burning so bright it must have blinded them to the sight of us crossing the lawn. Delphy on her stick, making speed, and me keeping up. I feel totally exposed, like if they had guns they could shoot us, no problem. But we finally make it to the ledge, clamber over it, and begin to climb the slope up into the woods.

The smoke is starting to thicken, but we can still see the Jeep waiting on the trail above us. We're about halfway up the slope—Delphy has more trouble on slanty ground—when the shouting starts.

At first I can't make out what they're shouting about, but then it becomes obvious. They've seen us. The biker bros come roaring across the lawn, the camp ablaze behind them, and zip along the ledge, looking for a way to get to us.

"You go ahead!" Delphy urges. "Get the Jeep started. I'll catch up."

"We're almost there."

I help her along. No way am I leaving her behind. I may be scared, but I'm not *that* scared. When Delphy falls flat on her face, I get her back on her feet. We keep going, yard by yard, struggling up the slope. Slipping, falling, doing it all over again. Focused on making it to the Jeep. Trying not to think about the craziness lurking behind us.

Delphy manages to throw her stick ahead. I've got her hand, and finally we're there.

She crawls into the Jeep, holding her stick in both hands, like a sword. I plug the distributor wire back in, slip behind the wheel, and press the starter pedal.

The engine catches first try.

As I slip the shifter into first gear, I take a look down the slope and see something that just about stops my heart.

The biker bros have found the planks we propped on the ledge, and they zoom across, side by side. Working their way up the slope as fast as they can, skidding around trees and flying high over rocks and protruding roots. Intent on reaching us, the sooner the better.

I feel like a rabbit with a pack of wolves bearing down.

"Sam!" Delphy screams, snapping me out of it.

I let out the clutch and press the accelerator pedal to the floor, running up through the gears. We're hitting forty miles an hour, flat out, and it's all I can do to keep us from flying off the trail. Dirt bikes can go eighty miles an hour, so there's no way to outrun them. I figure they'll be on us in thirty seconds or less.

Hunkered down in the passenger seat, Delphy starts to cough. A moment later, I'm coughing, too, and my eyes are stinging.

I risk a glance behind. A cloud of dense black smoke roils behind us like a breaking wave. The wind is strong at our backs, and the smoke from the fire is catching up even faster than the bikers. That's a good thing, but not if it means we can't breathe.

Seems like there's no way to get away from the smoke, other than to try and outrun it. I concentrate on maintaining maximum speed. We're flying over ruts, bouncing hard enough to make the steering wheel shudder like a living thing. Springs shriek with every bump. The Jeep was designed for terrain like this, but not at full speed.

We don't have a choice. Slowing down means dying from smoke inhalation, or at the hands of maniacs. Not a risk I want to take. So I concentrate on the trail ahead, on steering us safely through the turns. Nothing I can do about what's happening behind us; whatever lies down the road, that's my business.

We enter a long curve on the logging trail. The change in direction gives us a whiff of fresh air, and we gratefully fill our lungs. The forest is dense on both sides of the trail, and for a little while the scent of pine overpowers the stink of smoke.

The trees look like they'll be there forever, reaching to the sky. But soon the fire will change everything, reducing the landscape to ash. Do they know it, these mighty trees? Do they have any sense of what's coming?

Weird what you think about when you're trying to outrun a fire. When your brain is locked into what it means to be alive. When every moment is so intense that the colors are more vivid, and every bounce and rattle, every whiff of pine-sap, says you must find a way to survive. Even if you're the rabbit and the wolves are close behind.

"Sam!" Delphy shouts. "Do you hear that?"

Then I hear it, too. The banshee scream of dirt bikes at maximum velocity.

A moment later, they burst through the smoke and are instantly upon us.

36.

Road to Nowhere

In every car-chase movie I've ever seen, something impossible happens. Cars fly crazy distances through the air and land safely. They weave through wrong-way traffic like they're threading a needle. They go down flights of stairs, flip over, land right side up, and keep going. Like that. But in all those movies, I've never seen anything like my friend Delphy in action.

With an expression of fierce determination, she climbs into the back seat, clutching her walking stick. Crouches down like she's terrified and wants to keep a low profile. But when the first biker catches up and starts screaming, "You're dead! Stop the Jeep or die!" she suddenly leaps up, swings her stick, and *wham!* slams him so hard he flies off his bike and rolls along the trail like a rag doll.

Last thing I see before he's swallowed in the smoke, he's on his hands and knees, coughing up dirt. His bike is wrapped around a tree and totaled for sure.

You'd think the second biker would go back to help his fallen brother, but he doesn't. He's more intent than ever on trying to force us to crash. He comes up one side of us, standing on his pegs, and then veers away and comes up the other side, gunning his throttle. Darting at us, trying to rattle me. Daring me to try and hit him, and maybe lose control. All the time keeping just out of range of the walking stick.

The dude is a fantastic rider. Too bad he didn't concentrate on racing instead of setting fires.

Delphy keeps swinging, but he's clever, and either ducks or backs off at the last second, and she never connects.

After one last swing that misses, the stick slips from her hands and goes down between the seats. She paws around, trying to find it, and the rider veers closer, taking advantage. What if he leaps in and grabs the wheel? What then? If we let him have the Jeep, will he leave us alone?

But this is about more than taking the Jeep or crashing his brother. We've seen what they did, in two locations, and I'll bet there are more. I don't know if the brothers started the original fire, but for sure they've been helping it along.

The remaining rider edges in, gets a gloved hand on the side of the Jeep. And that's when Delphy grabs a gallon jug of water, and in one smooth motion, slams it upside his head. Like maybe dropping her stick was to fool him into coming so close. He goes over backward, landing hard in the dirt, and his bike goes straight up in the air and very nearly lands on him. Forks and wheels bent, frame twisted. The bike is finished, done.

I'm thinking, as he fades into the smoke, that if you come after my friend Delphy, you've got a long walk home.

———————————

After we're sure we're clear, and that they haven't miraculously revived the chase, like would happen in the movies, I slow it down, into second gear. Delphy scrambles back into the front seat and gives me a soft little punch in the shoulder. "We did it, Sam."

I baby the Jeep—and us—for a few miles. The smoke is far behind us. We've outrun the fire for the time being. The wind is still blowing hard at our backs, no doubt driving the flames, so we don't dare stop for a rest. Not for miles yet. But for the moment, we made it.

In the seat beside me, Delphy curls up, trembling. Like the experience finally caught up to her.

"You did good!" I tell her. "They were going to get us for sure!"

"I was so scared. Way more than I'm scared of the fire. Did you see their eyes? They were empty, like Halloween pumpkins with the candles blown out."

"Phat Freddy said people have died in the fire. It could be their fault."

Delphy nods. "Do you think they got away? Their bikes were wrecked for sure."

"I bet they're fine. They know this area like the back of their hand."

167

Delphy pauses, lost in thought for a little while. "Where are we? Any idea?"

"Far to the west is all I know. I'm sorry, but this seems to be the logging trail to nowhere."

She sits up and looks around. "It can't be a road to nowhere, Sam. I mean, what would be the point?"

We drive on, gaining ground for the next few miles as we head deeper into the wilderness. The logging trail gradually rises until we're going over thinly wooded hilltops. We glimpse low mountains in the smoky distance. I'm so into keeping on the trail, and being careful how I steer, that I forget to check the compass on the dash.

When I finally do check the compass, the surprise hits me like a punch to the gut. We'd been heading more or less west. Now we're heading east. It must have happened real gradual, but it freaks me out that I didn't notice.

"Do you smell that?" Delphy sits up straight.

"The logging trail has turned back on itself. So the wind is in our faces. That's why the stink of smoke is worse."

"What does that mean? Turned back on itself?"

"It means we're going the wrong direction." I'm sick to admit it. "We're heading back toward the fire."

37.

The End of the Trail

"How is that even possible?" Delphy wants to know. As if she's been napping and now she's wide-awake, demanding answers.

I shake my head. "It's not like we're on a major highway, heading in a certain direction. The logging trail wanders all over the place."

"Looking for logs." Delphy's face is scrunched up in concentration.

"For lumber. This trail goes where the trees are. It doesn't care about compass headings, or outrunning forest fires."

"Okay, I get it." She sighs. "Let me think. Turning around would be a bad idea because the other end of the trail has already been overrun by the fire, right?"

"Right."

"So no matter which way we drive, we're heading for the fire. Which means we're doomed."

"Maybe not." I try to sound upbeat. "Maybe the logging trail swings round to the west again. Some of this may be switchbacks."

"Switchbacks?"

"Think of a heavy truck loaded with tons of logs. It can't go straight up a hill. It can't do steep. So it weaves back and forth, gaining a little altitude with each turn. That's switchbacks. On a real, paved road they're very precise. But carving a logging trail through the woods? Not so much. All I know is, we gained altitude over the last hour or so. We're on top of the hills, not going around them like before."

"Is that good?"

"Maybe. I'm not sure. But we're more out in the open than we were in the deep woods. If a plane or helicopter goes over, they might see us."

Delphy snorts, her eyes angry. "As if. You know our problem? Nobody knows where we are, and nobody is looking. Nobody cares!"

"That's not true."

She sighs. "I know, I know. I'm just frustrated."

I figure we've got no choice but to see where the logging trail leads. I put the Jeep in gear, and sure enough, after fifteen minutes or so of winding along the hillside, we're headed west again. Switchbacks, no doubt about it. I try to imagine a fully loaded lumber truck trundling along in these ruts, and it reminds me how dangerous it can be, driving a big rig. One little mistake and you slip off the road and maybe flip over, trapped in your cab.

That reminds me of what happened to Dad in Afghanistan, so I try to banish those thoughts from my mind and concentrate on the trail ahead. *Keep to the ruts. Do not deviate. Concentrate on the task at hand, and the road will take care of itself.* What my father called his "three mantras," things he kept in mind that helped him drive safely, back when he was hauling pulpwood.

Every now and then, I glance over to check on Delphy. She has her arms crossed and looks miserable. Probably wishing she'd never gotten into the Jeep in the first place. If she'd stayed where she was in the woods, not far from the fire, maybe rescuers would have found her. Maybe it's my fault she isn't already home.

Following the logging trail seemed like a good idea, but what if it was a big mistake? What if instead of saving our lives, everything I've done has only made it worse?

"Sam? What's happening?"

Delphy's worried tone jerks me out of feeling sorry for myself. I start to pay attention to the landscape beyond the trail, and she's right, something has changed.

It's as if we're rising above tree level, away from the darkness of the forest. But that's not it. We're still in the low hills, nowhere high enough to be above tree level. The trail has widened into a large open area populated with skinny birch saplings. Thin enough so we can see for miles, way beyond the rolling hills to the fire itself. A great black scar that runs from horizon to horizon, fed by an orange line of fire driven by wind and fuel. Like an army of flames marching through a crack in the world.

171

"This hilltop? It was clear-cut a few years ago," I tell her. "See all those old stumps, with the birches growing up between them? That's what happens when you cut down all the trees. New ones grow back, and the first generation is usually something like birch, which is fast-growing."

Delphy looks at me impatiently, not the least bit interested in all the cool woodsy stuff I learned at camp. She wants to know what it means for us, right now.

"I'm sorry, but it looks like this is why the logging trail was built. All those miles. They wanted to bring rigs up here to harvest the really big trees."

"What are you saying?" Delphy grabs my arm as if she wants to shake the truth out of me.

A truth I don't want to speak, because it means I've been wrong all along.

"This is the end of the trail," I tell her softly. "This is as far as it goes."

38.

Because, Because, Because

The Jeep runs on gasoline. Step on the starter pedal and it'll keep going until it runs out of fuel. Me and Delphy, we've been running on hope, but now that tank is empty, and it's like the black clouds of the fire have entered our brains. We sit in the field of skinny birches and old stumps without speaking for a long time. Trying not to think, because there's nothing good to think about.

We can't go back the way we came, because the fire has overrun the logging trail. We can't stay where we are, because strong winds are blowing the fire in our direction. Soon enough it will climb this hill, sweep over the top, and burn its way back down into the thick forest that surrounds these hills in all directions.

If we stay where we are, we die. But where do we go? Running off into the forest doesn't make any sense, because if the fire isn't already there, it will be.

Delphy clears her throat. "Don't be too hard on yourself, Sam. What else could we do but follow the trail? It kept us alive for, what, three days?"

"Five days."

"Five days, see? You did good."

She reaches over to pat my hand. I snatch it away.

"Don't pretend!" I'm almost shouting. "I messed up. I was wrong all along. I was so sure the logging road had to meet up with a real road. Why was I so sure? Because I *wanted* it to. Like wishing would make it happen," I add, laughing bitterly.

"You did what you thought was best."

I get out of the Jeep and scuff through the underbrush. I want to be alone and Delphy knows it. She parks herself on one of the big stumps while I wander around, kicking at stuff.

I'm not mad at her. No way. I'm mad at myself. We nearly made it! All we had to do was bring the Jeep down the incline, across the survival camp lawn, and onto the gravel road. A state road was only seven miles away! We could have been on the road, a real road, last night. Armed ourselves with flashlights or something, to find the way.

Instead, we played it safe and decided to wait until dawn. Then the bikers showed up and ruined everything. Even without them, it might have been too late, the way the main fire was sweeping around the lake.

That was my mistake, not leaving while we had the chance. Because I was scared of driving at night without headlights. Because I didn't want to wreck the Jeep again. Because I was exhausted and wanted to sleep in a real bed.

Because, because, because. *Because* is going to get us killed. Unless we manage to find another path to an actual road. Something passable by the Jeep. But what are the odds, really, in an area so remote there's not a cabin or cottage visible from the hilltop?

Face it, we're doomed. Which is so scary I can hardly hold it in my head. That I might really die. That I'll be gone, leaving my mom alone in the world. What will she do with nobody to look out for her?

I'm wandering around the edge of the clear-cut area, half-heartedly trying to spot something that indicates a road might be nearby, when I happen to look through the birch saplings to the next few hills, which are about the same size and height as this one. Except they're fully wooded.

At first what I see doesn't make sense. A red-and-white needle, barely visible in the distance. Like a skinny arrow stuck into the top of the hill. It takes me a while to figure out what it is.

Could it be? Is it possible?

I hurry back through the clear-cut area, and find Delphy on the stump, sipping from a jug of water. She looks up with a tight little smile. "You done kicking rocks?" She studies my face. "Sam? You found something, I can see it in your eyes."

"This way. I'll show you."

She follows me to the edge of the clear-cut area and pushes a birch sapling out of the way so she's got a clear view of the hilltops.

175

I point. "What does that look like to you?"

She squints. "A radio antenna? But what good does it do?"

"It didn't just appear out of nowhere," I say. "Somebody had to build it. Had to bring in the pieces and put them together and raise the tower and stuff like that. So they needed a *road*."

Delphy breathes a sigh of relief. "Of course they did."

Then she gives me a hug that just about crushes my ribs.

39.

No Going Back

The hilltop with the radio antenna is less than a mile away, but with no clear path or trail to follow, it might as well be a thousand. Probably we could make it on foot, but without the Jeep and a real road out once we get there, there's no way to escape. Not with the huge, horizon-wide fire racing at us, driven by hot gusts of wind almost strong enough to knock us down.

I don't know how long we've got, exactly, but at this rate, the fire will sweep over these hilltops in less than an hour, at most. We haven't got time to clear a path, even if we had a way to cut down trees, which we don't. So we'll just have to give it a shot, and hope the old vehicle can find its way through the scraggly trees and bushes that cover the hillside.

"Hang on." I put the Jeep in gear. "We'll be going slow, but it'll be bumpy. If you feel us tipping over, try to throw yourself clear."

Delphy nods vigorously, but doesn't say a word. I don't have to tell her how dangerous this is, plunging down a steep hillside without a path or trail to follow. There's no going back once we head over the edge.

I pat the dashboard for luck. "Take care of us, dear lovely old Jeep, and we'll take care of you. That's a promise."

Over the edge we go. For the first hundred yards or so, the steep slope is relatively wide open, with only a few trees and stumps to avoid. I hardly have to touch the gas pedal as we roll over the rough ground, rocking side to side. Then, suddenly, we're tearing through low bushes that block our view. I try riding the brake, but it barely slows us down. Besides, if we slow down too much, we'll get stuck for sure.

Don't touch the gas or the brake, I decide. Concentrate on steering, on seeing what's beyond the next row of bushes.

"You're doing good!" Delphy shouts. "To the left, see that tree? Then you're clear!"

That's how we do it, all the way down the slope, me steering like a maniac with my hands welded to the wheel, Delphy shouting out which way to turn. Bushes and saplings smacking the sides of the vehicle as we go by, as if urging us along.

Suddenly we break through the underbrush, lurching onto a rock-strewn ledge. The Jeep starts to skid sideways. I steer into the turn and we straighten. Finally the tires get purchase on the slippery rock.

Back in control, I steer around the bigger boulders. Then there's grass under the wheels, and the ledge is behind us.

We're picking up speed, and Delphy is shouting out which way to go.

A grove of thin little saplings ahead, too many to avoid. We roll right through, mowing them down. Branches whip at us, trying to snatch us out of our seats. But we hang on. We keep going, bumping over hard ground and soft dirt, rolling through bushes, skidding around bigger trees and the occasional boulder that comes out of nowhere.

I'm so focused on steering that I don't really get it that we made it to the bottom of the slope until the Jeep slows down and starts to roll backward. I look over at Delphy. She's clinging to her seat with both hands. If her eyes were any bigger, they'd fall out of her face.

"That was interesting." She takes a deep breath.

Working our way slowly up the next hill is way less exciting, but it takes just as much effort. A couple of times we have to backtrack when the trees get too dense, but we manage. Finding our own switchback pathways when it gets too steep, and barging straight ahead whenever possible.

We finally get to the top of the hill. There isn't any part of me that doesn't hurt. My hands are so cramped I have to pry my fingers off the wheel. My legs ache and my butt feels bruised, but it's all worth it, because we can see the radio tower looming over us. Close up, it looks old and rusty. The cables that anchor it in place moan with the gusts of wind.

The air is thickening with the eye-watering stink of fire. Even if we couldn't see it—the line of black clouds closing in, the orange flames racing over the treetops—we'd know the fire wasn't far away.

We need to find a road, and fast.

The Jeep bumps over the rough meadow around the radio tower. Delphy's trying to stand up in her seat, searching for an opening that might indicate a road. Neither of us is saying much because we're running out of time. I don't know what's going through Delphy's head, but my brain is thinking crazy thoughts. Like if we don't find a road, maybe we can climb to the top of the tower to get away from the fire. Might survive if the flames sweep through fast, but it's just as likely we'd end up like chunks of barbecue.

I know, disgusting, but I can't help imagining the worst.

We roll through the meadow, dead grass crunching under the tires, and steer around a small stand of scrawny spruce trees. Eyes watering as the smoke gets worse. Desperate for a road. At this point, any kind of road will do, even another road to nowhere, just so we can stay alive for a while longer.

"Hey!" Delphy shouts, pointing. "Over there!"

What she spotted isn't a road, it's a building. A square, flat-roofed building made of cinder block, sitting in the middle of a clearing. White paint peeling and blistered on the sides, but the bold lettering over the door is still clearly visible.

"It's him." I'm astonished. "Phat Freddy."

Delphy shakes her head. "He must have got rescued some-how. He said it was his final broadcast, and that was last night. He's gone."

"Maybe not." I lean on the horn.

40.

Ride of the Falconries

The man who stumbles out of the cinder-block building is a lot older than I expected from the sound of his voice. He's got a short white beard and a long white ponytail that goes almost to his waist. The ponytail reminds me of Willie Nelson, but Phat Freddy has a potbelly, and that spoils the resemblance.

Wheezing from the smoke, he barely makes his way across the unpaved parking lot. "Oh my Lord!" he exclaims, his red-rimmed eyes taking us in. "You sent me two angels in a Jeep!"

"Is there a road?"

"Access road! Hasn't been paved in years!"

"Hop in! Show us the way!" I have to shout, because the roar of the approaching fire has gotten so loud. It's not a normal sound. More like the trees are screaming. Must be my imagination, because trees don't scream, do they?

Freddy scrambles into the back.

We tear around the building and sure enough, there's an old, pothole-riddled road just wide enough for the Jeep. My heart soars—we've got a chance!

From the back seat, Freddy leans forward, pitching his radio voice to be heard above the roar of the approaching fire.

"Thanks for the ride, kids! Figured I was a fried chicken for sure!"

"Everybody hang on!" I yell. "I'll be going as fast as I can, and the road looks bad!"

We're just starting down the bumpy access road when the fire sweeps up over the hillside, igniting the meadow and the underbrush and the stand of scrawny pines all at once. More an explosion than a fire. Like the world was doused in gasoline, and God was holding the match.

But the only thing in my head is trying to stay alive. Too late to get ahead of the fire, so we have no choice but to find a way through it. The access road is steep, and the potholes are deep. Steer hard, yanking the wheel to avoid breaking an axle. All around us, trees ignite from the top down, jumping from crown to crown. As if the wildfire has been lifted into the air, into the treetops.

A wave of scalding heat makes it hard to breathe.

"Give me your under shirt!" Delphy shouts at Freddy. "Quick!"

I can't quite see what she's doing, but a moment later, she ties a water-soaked rag over my mouth and nose. Then does the same for herself and Freddy.

We probably look like scruffy bandits, but it really helps. Breathing through a damp cloth is the best we can do under the circumstances.

Maybe you think it's brave, what we did. But courage had nothing to do with it. We were terrified and we kept going because we had no choice. Down that winding access road, avoiding potholes. Keeping as close to the middle as possible because fire is racing down both sides, exploding from tree after tree.

I may have been screaming, not that anyone noticed or cared. Screaming as much in anger as fear. Because I couldn't help thinking about what happened to my dad when the Hummer hit his truck in Afghanistan. How the gasoline tanker he was driving rolled off the shoulder of the road, turning the rig upside down. How he was trapped in the cab as the gas poured out and then exploded.

They say he was probably unconscious when it happened, but nobody knows for sure. Mom didn't want me to hear the details, or read the report from his company, but I had to know. I had to, because my imagination made it even worse than the report, which concluded he perished in less than thirty seconds.

Thirty seconds can be an eternity if you're inside a fire. Believe me, I know. That's probably how long it takes to get all the way down the access road, which is only a few hundred yards.

It finally levels out at the intersection with a paved road.

I scream, "Which way?" and Freddy points to the left. We barrel down the middle of the road—a real road, not a trail—hitting fifty miles an hour on the speedometer. Pedal all the way to the floor, with me hunched over the wheel, urging it to go even faster. That old machine purring like it's young and brand-new. Maybe it thinks we're on a battlefield in Korea, but wait, machines can't think, can they?

This one can, in my imagination, because it was like the Jeep took over. I was holding the wheel, but the Jeep was steering because I was so distracted by the exploding trees that I couldn't think straight.

I could hear Delphy and Freddy chanting, "Go! Go! Go!" but it was like something in a dream. Like they were part of a soundtrack my dad used to play, a thrilling passage that for years I thought was called "Flight of the Falconries." I used to imagine flocks of falcons diving into battle, claws outstretched, but it was never falcons at all. It was something from old Norse folktales called Valkyries. Female angels of death who ride into the battlefield, deciding who will live, and who will die, and who will go to heaven.

I wasn't ready for heaven. None of us were. We wanted to live, and it was the Jeep that helped us, never hesitating as that seventy-year-old engine hit RPMs that under normal circumstances would make it seize up. That day it ran cool and smooth, and somehow it kept accelerating—okay, that was me, standing on the pedal as we headed downhill—and we flew down that road something beautiful, catching up with the flames and passing them, blowing through clouds of hot black smoke and emerging unscathed.

Well, not quite. Burning cinders lit my hair on fire again, and Delphy jumped to put out the flames with her bare hands, shouting that we're going to make it, just keep going, you're doing great, you crazy little brother! Go! Go! Go! And I'm driving through the pain and the fear and coming out the other side.

Even now I have no idea if it was me or the Jeep that found our escape route. All I remember is that the road ended and the fire was catching up, surrounding us. We came off the paved road at sixty miles an hour, practically airborne, and then we were bouncing over a hard, grassy surface. I remember a couple of cottages flashing by and knew we were close to a lake, but I couldn't see it through the seething clouds of hot black smoke.

If we'd stopped on the shore, we'd have been toast, like all those cottages and cabins. But we didn't. The Jeep never slowed down, and when the wind blew the smoke away, just for a second, there it was, right in front of us.

A long dock heading straight out into that beautiful lake.

A long dock that was as good as a road, wide enough for the Jeep, and we tore down that dock at full speed, racing like no tomorrow as the fire swept around the lake, turning everything to flame, incinerating an entire evacuated village.

Maybe you heard how we flew off that dock and out into the lake and landed in the one and only spot where we had a chance to survive. Shallow enough so we couldn't drown, and situated in exactly the right place. The Loon Lake Miracle Spot, they called it. The one place in the entire lake where the air was far enough from the fire so it was possible to breathe without searing our lungs.

The water was only about three feet deep, but that was just enough to protect us, and to keep us cool as the rest of the world went up in flames. Two kids and an old man, sitting in a sunk Jeep with the water up to our armpits, laughing our heads off, glad to be alive.

How cool is that?

41.

This Is the End, My Friends

Delphy told me later that I was yelling, "Nobody dies! Nobody dies!" all the way down the mountain. Honestly, I don't remember that part. All I remember is the tops of the trees exploding like artillery shells, and the flash of super-hot air that wanted to melt us, and Freddy clinging to the Jeep like his life depended on it. Which of course it did. They say at the core of a crown fire the temperature can exceed 1,400 degrees Fahrenheit. One breath of air that hot and you're dead.

Later I learned that the Great North Woods Fire was the largest ever in the history of the state, and that at times it spread almost as fast as the dry windstorms that pushed it. All we knew that day was that the fire kept chasing us, and no matter how fast we raced to get away, it was faster catching up.

They tried to make out like I was a hero. Ha! Some hero. I was scared the whole time, from the very first day. There were lots of real heroes in the Great North Woods Fire. The long-haul trucker who drove his rig through ten miles of blazing highway to rescue his wife and children. That team of volunteer firefighters from Belfast who died trying to evacuate

189

those people who had taken refuge in the church cellar. Dozens of real heroes. Hundreds, probably, and most of their stories were never heard.

Personally, if a thing can be a hero, that old Jeep deserves a medal. By the way, the grandson of the man who owned the Jeep towed it out of the lake and had it completely rebuilt and presented to his grandfather, Captain Aldrich Brown, U.S. Army (Retired), on his ninetieth birthday. I know because I was invited to the birthday party. The old man looked so much like the young man in the photograph it was eerie. I guess running a logging operation for forty years keeps you in shape, because his old uniform still fit! The coolest thing was that after Captain Brown climbed into the Jeep to try it out, he saluted me.

And then he handed me the ownership papers.

That's right. The Jeep is in our garage, under a dust sheet, waiting for me to turn sixteen. As for Delphy, we talk all the time, and we see each other whenever. Yesterday she told me she was in love with some guy she met on line—in the grocery store, ha ha, is how she put it.

However it happened, good for her.

We were both relieved to hear that the dirt bikers survived and were arrested for arson. Charles and James Binney, who destroyed dozens of homes and helped the wildfire spread, and whose hatred of outsiders landed them in jail.

Good riddance, I say.

Oh yeah, you're probably wondering what happened with

190

my mom. That's a really long story, but the short version is, at the height of the fire she promised herself that if I survived, she'd complete rehab. Which she did. She's back home now. Managed to keep her job at the physical therapy clinic, too, and has really thrown herself into it, helping other people. Says it takes her mind off feeling sorry for herself, and that's a good thing. When she's not working or looking after me, she's out in her garden, weeding like crazy and bringing it back to life. Today a rosebush she thought was dead started to bloom.

It's been a long time since I've seen her so happy.

The truth is, she's still pretty shaky about what happens next. I keep telling her, Mom, nobody knows what happens next until it happens. All we can do is take it one day at a time.

Afterword: About Wildfires

I first heard about the devastating effects of wildfires from my mother. She had been a college student in Boston in the fall of 1947. That's the year Maine burned from the mountains to the sea, and the smoke from those fires tinged the skies all over New England. Desperate for help, the state of Maine sent trucks to Boston to round up young men willing to join the battle. Hundreds did, but despite their best efforts, the fires were out of control. They swept through coastal towns like Bar Harbor, to the north, and destroyed most of Shapleigh and Waterboro, to the south. An eight-mile wall of flames threatened to reduce the community of Kennebunkport to ash. Hundreds of homes were lost, and the forests of Maine were changed forever, with effects that still linger into the present century.

Later, friends of mine enlisted in hotshot crews in Montana, and they shared harrowing tales of their fight to contain fires that threatened to engulf the Bitterroot National Forest. They explained that going up against the Montana wildfires required courage, physical strength, strategy, and a certain amount of luck, much of it dependent on weather conditions.

Wildfires do not discriminate. They can erupt anywhere, if the conditions are right. In 2017, wildfires broke out in all fifty states. What sets them off? The vast majority are caused by humans. Drought and extreme weather conditions make fires much more likely, and one spark can turn a tinder-dry forest or grassland into a full-blown conflagration. Millions of acres of forest, and thousands of homes and structures, are lost to wildfires every year—and people lose their lives, including firefighters and other first responders. The U.S. Forest Service employs as many as ten thousand wildland firefighters during fire season, and they are joined by thousands of state and local firefighters. They all have the same mission: to save the lives of those threatened by fire, to prevent or contain wildfires, and to save structures when possible.

Firefighters use many strategies to stop wildfires. Early detection can help manage the damage. On the ground, firefighters work tirelessly to stop the fire by hand, using chain saws, shovels, and other equipment to remove fuel from the path of the advancing flames. They use water trucks and hoses to wet down grass and trees in the path of the fire, and homes are sprayed to save them. As embers blow, firefighters try to prevent new outbreaks. The challenges can be unpredictable, overwhelming, and extremely dangerous. Fire trucks, bulldozers, and other big machines may be brought in. Large wildfires can also be fought from the air with planes and helicopters that drop fire retardant or scoop water from lakes or other bodies of water. Some "Super Scooper" aircraft can dump as much as 1,600 gallons per flight. When a fire can't be otherwise reached, "smoke jumpers" sometimes parachute in. Their supplies are dropped nearby. More than 250 smoke jumpers fought fires in 2017.

Three elements are needed for fire: fuel, oxygen, and a spark to set it off. Under certain conditions, wind and flames combine into a fire tornado. A big wildfire makes its own weather, sometimes creating hurricane-force winds. In a large fire, flame temperatures can exceed 2,100 degrees Fahrenheit. Fires can also spread at incredible speed, and wind can blow them any direction. Multiple reports said the 2018 Camp Fire in California was blown by wind gusts approaching 50 miles per hour, and *60 Minutes* reported that "at one point the fire was spreading at a rate of one football field per second."

Wildfires are not new. Around the planet, there are many types of fires, and they have burned for hundreds of millions of years. Some wildfires occur naturally and are beneficial to the ecosystem involved; certain plants, for example, depend on fire for reproduction and healthy growth. However, the current pattern of more fires, longer fires, and bigger fires has been extremely destructive. In 2017, the states with the most wildfires were Texas, California, North Carolina, Georgia, Missouri, Florida, Mississippi, Montana, Arizona, and Oregon. The states with the most acres burned were Montana, Nevada, California, Texas, Oregon, Idaho, Alaska, Oklahoma, Kansas, and Arizona. Experts have many theories to explain the trend of larger, more frequent fires in much of the U.S., but overall, the cause seems to be a combination of extreme weather cycles, an increase in drought, and stronger winds to fan the fires.

How we manage forests—and fires—is also a factor. But however you explain it, the number of acres burning is steadily going up, up, up.

If your family lives in the path of a possible wildfire, the more you can learn about fires—and the more you can prepare—the better. There are things you can do that may well save your life.

As you can see, wildfires are complex, and surviving them can be very challenging. What would happen if you suddenly found yourself trapped in a wildfire—and, like Sam, you had no phone, and no rescue team searching for you? What would you do?

A Few Survival Tips
for You and Your Family

MAKE A PLAN

Determine the best routes for evacuation—ahead of time, if possible. Know where you'll go. Decide what to take with you, and what must be left behind. If fire is coming your way, get out quickly. Don't be like Sam and run back for your phone! In the event of fire in your house or building, have a place outside where you all know to meet.

KNOW YOUR ESCAPE VEHICLE

Try to learn about wildfire conditions. It can be very helpful to get in the habit of parking so that the vehicle is facing the direction of escape. Keep the tank full. If your electricity fails, you may be able to use your car to charge your phones and devices.

PACK YOUR VALUABLES

Gather up essential paperwork—such as passports, insurance company contact numbers, and personal financial information—and keep them in a sealed bag ready to grab at a moment's notice. Cash, credit cards? Food, water? Make a list of things you may need to grab quickly (including keys!). A handy suitcase or bag should contain a change of clothing and an emergency supply of medicine.

HAVE A PLAN FOR YOUR PETS

Keep carriers and crates handy, as well as a backup supply of pet food and pet medication.

WILDFIRE ALERTS

Download local alert apps to your cell phone. Most "fire-danger" states have such programs. If possible, pack a wind-up emergency radio and flashlights. In some fires, Wi-Fi is completely knocked out along with all electricity. Keep in touch with your neighbors and help everyone share information. Just knowing the location of the fire—and the direction it's moving—may save your life.

In addition to observing these very basic survival tips, learn as much as you can about fires, evacuation, and safety. You will discover that even a small amount of investigation will teach you many more things you may need to know. What is the likelihood that a wildfire might happen near you—or near your loved ones? What questions do you have? Most can be answered with a little basic research, using your library and search engines. Knowledge and preparation may well give you the power to survive—and to help others!

USEFUL SOURCES

Hundreds of articles, interviews, books, and websites were used to research the wildfire information in this book. Wildfires occur all over the world, and a vast amount of information is available. You might find the following sources useful:

US Forest Service: Public Fire Information
https://www.fs.fed.us/science-technology/fire/information

US Forest Service: Wildland Fire
https://www.fs.fed.us/managing-land/fire

Statistics: National Interagency Fire Center
https://www.nifc.gov/fireInfo/fireInfo_statistics.html

Wildfires: National Centers for Environmental Information (NOAA)
https://www.ncdc.noaa.gov/sotc/fire

About Wildfires: Smokey Bear
https://smokeybear.com/en/about-wildland-fire

How to Prepare for a Wildfire: FEMA.gov
https://www.fema.gov/media-library-data/1409003859391-0e8ad1ed
42c129f11fbc23d008d1ee85/how_to_prepare_wildfire_033014_508
.pdf

Wildfires: Ready.gov
https://www.ready.gov/wildfires

What to Do if You Become Trapped Near a Wildfire: Ready for Wildfire
http://www.readyforwildfire.org/What-To-Do-If-Trapped/

Learn Wildfire Safety Tips: *National Geographic*
https://www.nationalgeographic.com/environment/natural-disasters
/wildfire-safety-tips/

University of California, Forest Research, and Outreach: Wildfire
https://ucanr.edu/sites/forestry/Wildfire/

Fleeing the California Wildfires: What to Take and When to Evacuate
https://www.nytimes.com/2017/12/07/us/fire-evacuation-california
.html

About the Author

Newbery Honor author Rodman Philbrick grew up on the coast of New Hampshire and began writing novels at the age of sixteen. As is often true of aspiring writers, Philbrick wrote for many years before finally publishing his first book. In fact, he wrote eight or nine unpublished novels for adults, and during those years, he also worked as a roofer, carpenter, longshoreman, and boatbuilder.

Eventually he turned to the genre of adult mystery and suspense thrillers and published his first novel at the age of twenty-eight. Over the next dozen years, he published fifteen of them, several under a pseudonym.

Freak the Mighty, Philbrick's first book for young readers, was published by the Blue Sky Press/Scholastic in October of 1993. Among its many honors, the book won the California Young Reader Medal and was chosen by the American Library Association as a Best Book for Young Adult Readers. Now considered a classic, it has sold more than four million copies and was made into a 1998 Miramax movie, *The Mighty*. Philbrick wrote a sequel, *Max the Mighty*, because "so many kids wrote to me suggesting ideas for a sequel that I decided I'd better write one myself before someone else did."

Philbrick's rip-roaring historical novel about an inveterate teller of tall tales, *The Mostly True Adventures of Homer P. Figg*, is set during the Civil War, and was a 2010 Newbery Honor Book. The Kennedy Center commissioned a theatrical production of the book, which premiered in 2012. Another novel that examines American history is Philbrick's *Zane and the Hurricane: A Story of Katrina*, about Zane Dupree and his dog, Bandit, who are trapped in New Orleans just as Hurricane Katrina hits the city. This dramatic survival tale is both heroic and poignant, educating readers about an unforgettable catastrophe. Among its many honors, *Zane* was on the Texas Bluebonnet Award Master List.

Always suspenseful and filled with fascinating details, Philbrick's novels are also celebrated for their depth and heroism. *The Young Man and the Sea* is the powerful tale of a boy trying to save his grieving father by taking a desperate fishing gamble out at sea. *School Library Journal* praised its "heart-pounding suspense" and named it a Best Book of the Year. For young adults, *The Last Book in the Universe* is set in a dangerous future where reading and writing are a thing of the past, but when a young gang member discovers books, he sparks a rebellion. It was an ALA Best Book for Young Adults and a YALSA "100 Best of the Best Books for the 21st Century." Philbrick's 2016 *The Big Dark*, about social dysfunction that erupts after a solar flare wipes all electricity off the planet, was a "Recommended Page-Turner" by the *Horn Book*.

From coast to coast, Philbrick engages young readers with stories about ordinary children who are suddenly faced with seemingly insurmountable obstacles—and must summon up courage they don't even know they have. For this ability to connect with readers, Philbrick's books have been given awards and nominations by more than thirty-five states—often multiple times.

For a number of years, Philbrick thought the devastating Great Fire of 1947, in which his home state of Maine burned from the mountains to the sea, would make an interesting subject for a survival adventure story. But the increasing number of wildfires nationwide convinced him to set the story in the present. After a period of research into how changing climate has made fires more frequent and more dangerous, he started writing *Wildfire*, in February of 2017.

On November 8, 2018, *Wildfire* was in its final stage of editing. That day, massive wildfires broke out in California. The Camp Fire and Woolsey Fire both raged out of control, much like the wildfire that chases Sam. Many people lost their lives, their loved ones, their homes, and more. About this novel, and the rampant wildfires that are now being called "the new normal," Philbrick says, "I wish this book was fiction, but it keeps coming true."

Rodman Philbrick currently divides his time between Maine and the Florida Keys.

Looking for more action-packed, edge-of-your-seat survival? Keep reading for a sneak peek at Rodman Philbrick's WILD RIVER.

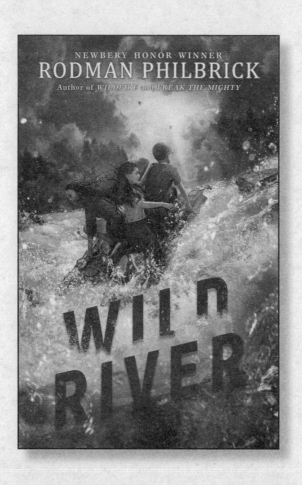

Prologue

The blamers and the shamers have it all wrong about the horrible events at Crazy River. Nobody knew what was going to happen, so it's nobody's fault. A free trip to Montana to experience a white-water rafting adventure? Who could say no to that? Not me, for sure. And not any of the other kids in Project Future Leaders. Which was some kind of joke, or I wouldn't have been selected to participate. Because, believe me, nobody looks at me and says, "Now, there's a born leader!" They see Daniel Redmayne, a pale, skinny kid with glasses and a lucky Red Sox cap. A middle schooler who would rather write a fantasy story or draw a cartoon than do his homework. A student who teachers say needs motivation, and often fails to participate in class. *Lost in his own world*, one of them wrote on my last report card. So, not a likely pick for anything.

Maybe the others were more qualified, and I was just a mistake. Or that's what I thought at the time. Whatever, there were five of us in the van that day, heading for a river somewhere deep in the Montana wilderness. Me,

Deke, Tony, Mia, and the quiet girl with the bouncy dreads, Imani. Plus two adult supervisors, or "guards," as Deke liked to joke. Yuk, yuk. And no matter how unfunny, you have to laugh at Deke's jokes or he'll pound you. Sky Hanson, the rafting guide, was driving. Cindi Beacon—yes, *that* Cindi Beacon—was there for supervision and inspiration. As you probably already know, she was the top striker for the US national team that won the last World Cup, and for sure the most famous person any of us had ever met. I know girls who have her poster on their walls. Boys, too.

Expensive people, expensive trip. Good thing it was sponsored by Byron James, the famous billionaire inventor. What was he thinking? Probably that our new regional middle school was being named for him, and this was his way of saying thanks.

Big mistake, as it turned out. Huge. But he had no way of knowing how it would turn out, or how many of us would die.

Day One

1.

Crazy River, Here We Come

It starts out as the best day ever. For a kid from a small town in New Hampshire, Montana is freaking awesome. The place has mountains high enough to scratch the pure blue sky, ranches half as big as the entire state of Rhode Island, and grizzly bears and mountain lions and herds of wild buffalo. And the best part? They still have real live, actual cowboys. I mean, think about it!

Deke pretends to be bored, but most of us kids are staring out the van windows like we can't believe our eyes. Our white-water guide, a really friendly dude with a bushy blond beard and a matching ponytail, has been pointing out the sights. Mostly mountains and canyons with strange names, and glints of creeks and rivers way down in the steep ravines.

"Couple more miles," he says cheerfully. "Sorry our primary destination didn't work out, but the Crazy, you have my word it will deliver the goods."

Crazy is the name of the river we're heading for, and we've got our fingers crossed that it won't be as low and dry as the first choice. Can't have a white-water adventure without white-water rapids, right? So it's worth driving a hundred miles farther into the wilderness for what Sky promises will be "the rafting ride of a lifetime."

Strapped into a seat in the third row, Mia raises her hand and waits until one of the grown-ups spots it in the rearview. "Yes?"

"When do we eat?"

Sky shakes his head and chuckles. "Girl, you must have a hollow leg. We had a big breakfast, and you had a big lunch. Two helpings of ice cream, as I recall. To answer your question, next meal will be over a campfire on a sandy beach. Until then, you'll find snacks in the blue cooler."

Mia makes an impish face. I doubt she's really hungry. Just making herself known. Deke gives her a sullen look. She crosses her arms and ignores him. Tony sleeps with his head leaning against the window, oblivious as usual. And our famous soccer player, Cindi Beacon, the one they call Tiny Dancer because of her size and her moves, is playing a game on her phone. No cell reception out in the wilderness, or she'd probably be reporting back to her agent, which she does a lot. From what I can tell, it's pretty complicated being a celebrity. Still, she's really nice and down-to-earth, and doesn't brag about being famous.

The van turns onto an even smaller road, more like a rutted trail. We left the pavement long ago, but this is a lot bouncier.

"Over there!" We strain to see where Sky is pointing. "Through those trees. Big Medicine Dam, one of the oldest in the state. Built for purposes of irrigation, and retrofitted for flow control in the 1950s. Some want to tear it down and free the river. Others think it needs to be rebuilt for safety. All we care is that it feeds the Crazy."

The van comes to a stop, seemingly at no place in particular, surrounded by forest.

Once we're all out, Sky claps his hands together. "We'll hike down from here. Cindi and I will portage the raft. Everybody else, take a pack. And while you're strapping up, we'll give the sat phone another try."

Sky and Cindi bend over the satellite phone, punching buttons and shaking their heads in frustration. After a brief discussion, they nod in agreement.

Sky strides back to us, clearing his throat. "Listen up, people! We had to make a decision. Base was duly notified about abandoning our first destination. But the phone is still down—looks like the battery croaked—so we can't contact them to let them know the Crazy is our final choice, understood? It's not as if we'll be alone on the river. Bound to cross paths with other tour groups, who are likely to have a working sat phone. In light of that, we have decided to proceed with our plan to raft the Crazy, and make contact later."

We all cheer, even Deke. Crazy River, here we come.

2.

Why They Call It Crazy

The hike down to the riverbed would be tough even without the packs. The trail is steep and twisty and the big pack feels like I'm top-heavy, and if I'm not careful, I'll tip over backward. I'm not the only one. Imani really does fall over, and when Deke laughs and makes fun of her, Sky makes him take her pack, too.

"This is a team effort," he says, very firm. "One of us falls, we pick our teammate up. Do whatever is necessary to preserve the team. Understood?"

Deke smirks but agrees. Sky is really nice and everything, but you get the idea it wouldn't be smart to make him mad. I'm worried that if Deke doesn't stop being such a jerk, he's going to ruin it for the rest of us.

When we finally get down to river level, there's a lot of work to do. Sky inflates the bright red raft and prepares it for launch. When it's ready, Cindi helps us stow and secure the packs, which contain all the food and gear we'll need for the three-day journey. Then she takes charge of making sure our bulky life jackets are adjusted and the chin straps on our helmets are fastened. I make sure the elastic strap on my glasses is tight.

Just before we climb into the raft, I finally get a chance to check out the scenery. Which is spectacular. There are high mountains all around us, with peaks like the points of a crown. Awesome. The clear mountain water, rushing around rocks and boulders, sounds like a distant crowd cheering. Across the river, tall fir trees line the water's edge like a row of dull green sentries. The ravine walls are higher and steeper than I expected, especially on the opposite shore. And it's just us. Not another raft in sight. Feels like we're all alone in the world. Us and the river and the unspoiled scenery. Not a bad feeling, and just scary enough to be exciting.

One by one, as our names are called, we pile into the big raft. Sky passes out paddles and shows us how to dip the blades and pull, but not too deep. "First rule of raft club, stay in the raft! Okay, for purposes of steering, you will be divided into two teams, left and right. Deke, Tony, and Cindi, you are Team Blue. Mia, Daniel, Imani, and me, we are Team Red. Got it? Today I'll be the raft commander and shout out directions. Okay? Everybody good? Here goes! Shove off!"

The current sweeps us away from shore, and the big raft starts spinning. Sky finally gets us pointed in the right direction by shouting "Red" or "Blue." At first I'm afraid to use my paddle—I really, really don't want to fall out of the raft—but then I start to get the hang of it.

It's fun!

At the first turn, we're almost swept up onto the rocky shore. At the last moment, we manage to get the raft back into the middle of the river. "Well done!" Sky exclaims. "You're getting the hang of it. Two more turns and we'll find the rapids. Or they'll find us!"

He explains this is how the river got its name. So many crazy twists and turns.

We manage to keep the raft centered through both turns, and then, suddenly, we start to pick up speed, like we're sliding down a slippery ladder. Going faster and faster. I hear it before we see it, the roar of the white-water rapids.

A second later, the bottom of the world seems to drop away. Waves, spray, big rocks, they all blur together. I'm instantly soaked from head to foot, and that's fun, too. Like the coolest ride in the coolest water park ever. The raft bobs and tips, and a couple of times it almost flips over. Or that's what it feels like. I think most of us are screaming, partly in terror and partly for the sheer fun of it. And we're all improving with the paddle work. The only one not cheering is Imani, but from the way she handles her paddle, I'm guessing this isn't her first rafting experience.

Sky has his hands full keeping us upright. Suddenly we're spinning backward and it's all I can do to stay in the raft, let alone follow Sky's shouted instructions.

"RED RED RED!"

He's digging like mad with his own paddle. We're heading right for a huge white boulder, waves breaking all around it. I don't know what to do, or how to help. We're doomed for sure. But somehow Sky shoves us off, and then we're spinning the other way and I get a face full of water that makes it hard to see.

Next thing I know, we're out of the rapids and slowing down as the river widens. Our screams turn to cheers.

We made it!

And maybe if we'd stopped right there, all of us would have survived.

More award-winning novels from Newbery Honor author
RODMAN PHILBRICK

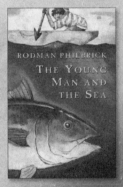